FRIENDS
OF ACPL

Chris

BY CAROL HOFF

COVER ILLUSTRATION BY ROBERT PATTERSON

Follett Publishing Company

Chicago

Library of Congress Catalog Card Number: 60-9368

FOURTH PRINTING

Follett Publishing Company
1010 West Washington Boulevard
Chicago, Illinois 60607

T/L 1175

To Ray

Chris

1

A New Home

Dad lay snoring gently, but Chris, in the bed across the room, was too worried to sleep. His whole mind and body ached with dread of starting school tomorrow.

How can Dad sleep like that when I'm so miserable? Chris wondered.

He lay stiff and straight with the blanket up to his chin and the cool night air flowing over his face.

It must have been an hour ago that Dad had turned out the light, opened the windows, and crawled into bed.

"Ummm, this feels good," he had said, sighing luxuriously. "It's been a long day. Reckon I'm the tiredest man in Texas! Hey, my mattress is fine. How's yours?"

"All right," Chris had answered. But he wasn't really comfortable in this strange bed. It felt hard and unyielding, lacking the cozy hollows of his mattress of the last three months.

The March full moon shone into the room, so bright it made Chris cover his eyes. It looked as big and shiny as the tin dishpan in the apartment in Premont.

Chris shielded his eyes by putting his arm over his forehead, and looked around the room, trying to get used to its strangeness. He saw the heap of their suitcases and the pile of towels and bedding near the dresser, the box packed with his airplane models and comic books on the table, and the tall stack in the corner made by Dad's golf clubs and rifle and his own Benjamin pump gun, baseball bat, and fishing rod.

The moonlight glinted on the mirror and on the knob of the door to the kitchen, and on the top can in the box of groceries on the kitchen table. They had been too tired to unpack tonight, but by bedtime tomorrow everything would be in its place on shelves or in drawers, and the apartment would look neat and bare, the way Dad liked it.

Dad and Chris had learned to travel light, because several times a year they had to be ready to move at a few hours' notice. Dad was a driller for Texray Oil Company, and as soon as one of their South Texas oil

10

wells was completed or abandoned, he had to move to another location and start a new one. The trouble was that every time they moved, Chris had to change schools.

And that was what was worrying Chris now.

But he and Dad had the moving business down to a fine routine, with none of the fuss and feathers the families with women always went through. Dad even used the same words each time they looked for an apartment. He had found just the right ones. Chris had a hard time to keep from laughing sometimes, for the landlady usually fell into the pattern perfectly, just as Mrs. Whittset, their new landlady, had done.

"I'm looking for an apartment for my son and myself," Dad would say, standing tall and lean and darkly handsome, with his hand on Chris's shoulder.

"Your wife won't be with you?"

"My wife died when Chris was four years old. We're used to keeping house by ourselves."

"But without a woman? I don't know!"

"We like to keep things spic and span. Army training, you know."

"But with a boy his age? I don't usually take children."

"Chris is past the destructive age," Dad would say. "I'll guarantee his good behavior."

Chris would stand quietly, forcing a pleasant smile.

But he would be thinking, "What does she expect me to do? Dig holes in her flower beds like a dog? Shoot out all her windows with a BB gun? Or draw pictures all over the wall paper?"

"Well, I just don't know," Mrs. Whittset had repeated.

"Please," Dad had said, turning on his charm. "It's late and I'm tired, and this apartment is the only one I've found that's the right size with two beds. So, please, won't you let us have this one?"

"Well, yes," Mrs. Whittset had agreed. "I'll let you have it for two weeks, anyway. We'll see then. But I warn you, I'm a busy woman, and I won't be able to help you with the boy."

"Oh, we don't expect it," Dad agreed quickly.

And so they had moved in before Mrs. Whittset could change her mind. Then they had eaten supper in a café and gone straight to bed.

And now Dad was snoring peacefully, but Chris couldn't sleep for worrying about tomorrow.

Suddenly he couldn't bear to be awake alone.

"Dad," he said urgently. "Dad!"

Dad woke with a start. "Huh?" he asked. "What's the matter?"

"Dad, I can't start school tomorrow," Chris said desperately.

"What do you mean, you can't start school?" his father answered. "Of course you'll start school tomorrow."

"But, Dad, I just can't. You don't know what it's like to start in a new school in the middle of the term."

"Don't be silly, Chris."

"I could get a job, Dad. I could carry grocery bags in a supermarket or get a paper route. In a few years I'll be big enough to work on the rig."

"What's got into you lately about school, Chris? You went through a routine like this when we moved to Alice. I know it's hard to change schools three or four times a year, but you've done it all your life. You know it's that way in the oil business. You know that as long as I'm a driller, we'll have to move every few months. What's different now?"

"Nothing, but —"

"Then what's this about no school? Do I cuss you out when you make low grades? Did I so much as blame you when you failed sixth grade last year?"

"No, but —"

"Well then, just get it in your head that you're going to school tomorrow. You're going on till you finish high school, and after that you're going to college."

"But, Dad!"

"No 'buts' about it. What if it is a little harder on

13

you than on the other kids? You're no sissy. You can take it. Now go to sleep. I've got to be out at the rig by six in the morning, and I'm tired. Good night."

"Good night," said Chris weakly. To himself he added, "But I reckon I am a sissy. I can't take it any more. I just can't!"

He thought about what starting to school would be like. If only there were another boy his age among the crew families. But all the kids were in high school or just babies. He'd have to go all alone.

He just knew what would happen. The kids would stare at him as if to say: "We'll show you what's what in a hurry!"

The teachers would look at him as if to say: "Why did they have to send you to my room? I've got too many pupils as it is!" New books he'd never even seen, and he'd be expected to know everything in the back chapters. But mainly the kids, glaring at him as if he were trying to butt in, or else ignoring him as if he were made of air. Either way, it made you feel so bad, so lonesome —

"Dear God," Chris prayed unhappily, "please don't make me go to school tomorrow! Please fix things so I won't have to go! Couldn't you maybe let the school-house burn down? Or let the teachers go on a strike? Or — or something? I'd even be willing to break my

14

leg if you couldn't think of anything else. But please, dear Lord, I don't want to go to school tomorrow!"

Two tears rolled from his wide-open eyes. He wiped them away impatiently and shut his eyes tight to keep more from coming. "Please, dear Lord," he repeated, "no school tomorrow! Please . . . no school! Please . . ."

The next thing he knew, the alarm clock was ringing and it was morning.

2

A Bad Start

Dad had to be out at the oil well by six o'clock. He always got up and ate breakfast quietly and set the alarm to wake Chris at 7:30, in time for school.

This morning, when Chris opened his eyes, he didn't know where he was for a moment. Then the dread of the night before swept over him, and he burrowed down into the covers again.

In the bright sunshine of the new day he realized that it was unreasonable to expect God to wreck a whole school just for him. He felt hopeless and forsaken.

But he dressed carefully. He put on his favorite pair of blue jeans, the ones faded just right, so that they

16

looked neither brand new nor too old, his red and black plaid shirt, and his cowboy boots.

"I'll show 'em I'm as good as they are," he told himself grimly, looking into the mirror. He saw a tall, thin boy, black-haired and gray-eyed, with a sprinkling of freckles on his tanned face. It was a handsome face, like Dad's, though there was a wistful look in the eyes and a sad downward twist to the lips. But it did not please Chris. He examined it critically, as if it were the face of a stranger. "Maybe it will help if I comb my hair," he decided.

When his hair was slicked down, he turned away from the mirror with a sigh and went into the kitchen. On the table, weighted down by a box of cereal and the sugar bowl, was a note from Dad. "Don't forget to take your report card and your book card. Good luck," it said.

There was bread ready to be popped into the toaster, milk, and crisp cereal. But Chris was not hungry. He poured a glass of milk, drank half of it, and made his bed in the neat army way to match Dad's. Then he put on his leather jacket, picked up his briefcase with his school supplies, and started for school.

Dad had driven around the evening before until they had found the school. It was four blocks down and two blocks to the right.

As he crossed the last street, Chris could tell he was much too early, so he kept walking straight ahead, as if he were going somewhere else. At every corner he crossed the street, so he could look back at the school. When he saw five big busses stop and pour out boys and girls, he turned back.

It wasn't a bad-looking school, he had to admit as he neared it once more. It seemed to be brand new, but there was grass on the lawn, and red geraniums bloomed in a long bed under the windows.

A group of girls played hopscotch on the walk, and some boys played leapfrog nearby. They stopped and looked at Chris appraisingly as he walked up.

"Hi," he said. His throat felt dry and tight.

"Hi," they answered, without expression.

"Can you tell me where the principal's office is?" Chris asked. The words didn't come out the way he intended them. He meant them to sound gay and friendly, but even he could hear that they sounded loud and gruff.

The biggest boy answered him. "Sure we know where the principal's office is. What do you think we are, a bunch of dumbbells?"

The others snickered appreciatively. "That's telling him, Jack," one of the boys said.

Chris set his lips in a straight line and marched on toward the steps. At the end of the walk one of the boys

18

stuck out a foot and tripped him.

A broken leg! thought Chris swiftly. But he was not hurt. He only stumbled and dropped his briefcase. Stiff with embarrassment, he picked it up and entered the building.

The principal's office was the first room to the right. He stood in the door timidly. A blur of teachers filled the office, laughing and joking. Chris stood unnoticed for a minute. Then the principal saw him. "Yes, young man?" he asked. "Out of the halls till the bell rings, you know."

"I'd like to enroll," Chris began. But it's not true, he thought. I'd like not to enroll! Aloud he said, "I mean I'm a new pupil."

"Oh," said the principal. "In that case, you may go into the office to your left and wait for me. I'll attend to you later."

Chris went into the room and sat down in the only chair except the one at the desk. It was a small room without a window. There was nothing to see but the bare desk and a filing cabinet, with a picture of George Washington hanging over it.

"Oh, Mr. Elson," one of the teachers said, "I wanted to ask you about —" Someone shut the door, and it was dark in the little room. Chris could hear only a murmur of voices. In a few minutes the bell rang, and there was

19

the sound of hundreds of boys and girls going through the halls in orderly fashion. Then everything was quiet again.

"The principal will send for me now," Chris thought and fumbled in his briefcase for his book and report cards. But time dragged on, and he sat there in the dark waiting.

He felt very lonesome. A lump came into his throat. "They've forgotten all about me," he decided. "I'll sit here in the dark till I suffocate." He imagined the scene when his father, frantic with grief, found his limp, lifeless body slumped in the chair.

Suddenly another thought struck him. Could this be God's way of answering his prayer? He felt beads of perspiration pop out on his forehead. "Dear Lord," he whispered, "I guess I really didn't mean I hated school that bad! Please don't let me die!"

He thought he was going to be sick. But nothing happened. He twisted and turned and saw a faint pattern of light on the wall behind him. He investigated and saw that it came from the ventilator twirling in the ceiling overhead.

"At least I won't suffocate," he said and drew a deep breath.

A bell rang, and then after a long time another. Still Chris sat in the dark, waiting.

"Should I open the door?" he wondered. But in imagination he could hear the principal say sternly, "Young man, I told you to wait for me." So he sat stiffly and waited.

He thought of the other times he had sat waiting in the principal's office. There was the day in Premont when he had talked back to Miss Baker. And the spelling examination in McAllen when he had copied from the girl in front of him. The time in Corpus Christi when he was in the second grade and got lost in the corridors of the big school. And the morning in Alice when he had been in a fight on the school grounds.

These were all sad, dismal times, and the memories filled him with shame and foreboding.

At last the door opened. The sudden light blinded Chris for a minute, but he stumbled to his feet.

"What on earth?" exclaimed Mr. Elson as he flipped on the light. "Oh, it's you, young man. Have you been sitting here in the dark all this time? I'm sorry, I really am! Something came up, and I forgot all about you. Why didn't you remind me?"

He sounded friendly, but Chris felt you never could be sure about principals. "I didn't know whether you'd want me to," he answered timidly.

"Well, give me your book card and your report card, and we'll fix you up in a jiffy," Mr. Elson said cheerfully,

21

beginning to fill in blanks as he spoke.

It was only a jiffy before he handed Chris four cards and a stack of books and sent him on his way. "You'll be in VI-3," he said, "the fifth door down the corridor to your right. Your teacher's name is Miss Margaret Mayes. If there is anything I can do to help, come to see me."

With a friendly pat on the back, he sent Chris on his way.

Now was the time Chris had been dreading the most, the moment when he would enter his new class and face his new teacher and classmates for the first time.

Outside the door marked VI-3 he stopped. Should he knock, or just open the door and walk in? Some schools wanted you to knock, others just to open the door and stand with hand raised until recognized. With the pile of books in his arms, he decided it would be better to knock.

But he could not bring himself to do so. He stood there, his throat tight, the palms of his hands wet, his heart pounding. He was afraid in his whole being. Why, oh why did he have to walk in and face some old hag of a cross teacher and a roomful of staring kids ready to be his enemies?

Mr. Elson came out of his office. He walked in the other direction, but at the sight of him, Chris knocked quickly. A boy shoulder-high to him opened the door, and Chris stepped into the room.

Standing at the blackboard was the teacher. She was the most beautiful girl Chris had ever seen. "Come in," she said, and her voice was like music.

Then he heard a wolf whistle, shrill and clear, and was horrified to know that the whistle came from his lips.

He saw the smile go out of Miss Mayes's eyes. He saw the whole class sit up straight with shock.

Miss Mayes took a step toward him. "Well, Mis-ter!" she said in cold surprise.

"I'm sorry," Chris stammered swiftly. "I didn't mean to. It was just that I was expecting some frumpy old hag, and then I saw you!" He could hear his voice too loud again. He could feel the blood rushing to his face.

Miss Mayes's eyes remained cold, but a smile twitched at her lips. "I'll accept your apology," she said sternly. "Put your books on that shelf. We have no free desks in the room, so you'll have to get one from the janitor."

Chris walked over and put his books on the shelf. He could feel eyes boring into his back. He couldn't stand it. He turned and handed Miss Mayes his registration card.

"Will someone go with me to help me with my desk?" he asked. What made his voice so loud?

No one answered. The whole room sat still, looking at him.

"Boys and girls," Miss Mayes said, glancing at his card, "this is Chris Gregory. Who will go with him?"

No one answered. The silence became unbearable. Chris turned to the door. "Never mind," he said gruffly. "I don't need any help."

A girl in a back seat stood up. "I'll help him," she said.

A girl! The insult of being helped by a girl! And a girl with straggly hair and a brace on her teeth! And when she walked down the aisle her petticoat showed!

"Never mind," Chris repeated.

"That's friendly of you, Nell," Miss Mayes said approvingly. "Show Chris the way."

Chris left the room, and Nell followed. He was trapped. There was nothing he could do.

School in Oakdale was going to be even worse than he had feared.

3

Trouble at School

Two nights later there was a knock on their apartment door just after supper. Dad was washing the dishes, Chris drying them. He went to the door, towel in hand.

"Oh, Miss Mayes," he said, without enthusiasm.

"Hello, Chris," said Miss Mayes. "I've come to get acquainted with your parents."

"I'll call Dad," said Chris. Then he remembered his manners. "Won't you come in?"

Chris went into the kitchen. "It's my teacher," he whispered.

"So I gathered," Dad whispered back. "Get me a shirt!"

"Please excuse our whispered conferences, Miss Mayes," Dad called. "But the truth is, you've caught me without a shirt to my back."

"Oh, I'm sorry," said Miss Mayes. "You see, it's a policy of the school for teachers to call on their students' parents, and since you all are newcomers I thought it would be friendly to come at once. I'll come back another time."

"Oh, no," said Dad. "I'll be right in."

"But if Mrs. Gregory isn't here —"

"Chris's mother died when he was four," Dad said.

"Oh, I'm sorry. I didn't know," Miss Mayes faltered.

"Not at all, not at all," Dad reassured her. "All the more reason why you and I should get acquainted."

Chris sat stiffly facing Miss Mayes. She looked too beautiful for the dingy room. She looked like a movie star in technicolor.

Dad came in. When he saw Miss Mayes, he whistled.

"Chris didn't tell me he had such a pretty teacher," he said.

Chris's heart stood still. But Miss Mayes laughed.

"Like father, like son," she said. "Did you know that Chris greeted me with a wolf whistle the day he entered my class?"

"Chris, you didn't!" said Dad in surprise. But he

wasn't angry. "Well, he's a chip off the old block," he said. "I'm glad to see that he has an eye for beauty. Along with the sterner virtues like arithmetic and grammar, I've tried to inculcate an esthetic appreciation of the finer things of life."

Chris didn't know exactly what they were talking about, but he was relieved, for Miss Mayes laughed again.

She looked away from Dad, around the room. Chris suddenly saw it with her eyes: faded wallpaper, limp curtains, table littered with model airplane junk. At least the beds were made and there were no clothes lying around.

Dad must have felt as he did. "A poor place," he said, "but my castle for the moment."

"Oh, Mr. Gregory," Miss Mayes exclaimed, "I didn't mean to be rude!"

"You're not, you're not," Dad assured her. "I know it's your job to learn the environment of your kids. Well, here you have it, broken home and all." He spoke lightly. Then his tone became suddenly serious. "But he has a deeply devoted dad," he said. "How's my son doing in school?"

Miss Mayes answered cautiously. "Well, I'm afraid he has problems. I don't think you like school too well, do you, Chris?"

"No, ma'am," Chris replied briefly.

"It's tough for a kid to have to change schools as often as Chris does," Dad said. "Did he tell you this is the third school this year? He had four last year."

"No, he didn't, but I saw from his registration card that you were an oil man, so I guessed." She stood up to go.

"Can't you stay longer?" Dad invited. "I'll make some coffee."

"No, thank you," said Miss Mayes. "I must go now. We want Chris to be happy at school, and this visit has helped me to understand him."

She came over and put her hands on Chris's shoulders. "Chris," she said, "you know that, don't you? You know that I'm your friend and ready to help you any way I can?"

"Yes'm," said Chris, and suddenly he meant it. "Yes'm," he repeated, smiling.

But school continued to be a pain, just a pain. And there was nothing Miss Mayes could do about it. VI-3 had ganged up against Chris, and he knew it.

They had decided to ignore him. In class, if they had to choose sides or call on one another, he was never chosen. No one ever asked for permission to speak to him.

It made him feel lonesome as a ghost. They even

looked at him as if there were nobody where he was sitting.

On the playground it was even worse. They never chose him to be in a game. If he tried to join in a ball game, they said there were too many players. If they played Dare Base, none of the boys ever chased him. He could run wherever he pleased without being caught, and if he tried to rescue someone, the prisoner always darted toward the other side of the pen just as he reached out to touch him. He might have been made of air.

No one came to see him after school. After a few days he couldn't stand it any more. "Hey," he would cry, jumping from his seat in class, "choose me! I'm the best speller in this whole room!"

At recess he would yell, "Choose me! I'm the best fielder in this school!" or "You can use my mitt if you choose me!"

But they didn't choose him.

It was humiliating. Humiliating and lonely. He dreamed about it at night. VI-3 was always a bright, laughing group, gaily riding a merry-go-round, and he was nothing, just a black mass of nothing, looking on. And when he tried to get on the merry-go-round, all the little horses would snort and run away and the music box would play a jangly tune, till they set up a new merry-go-round just out of his reach.

He couldn't stand to be so alone. He would make them notice him. So he began to get permission to speak to one or another of the boys. "Go away," they would say, "or I'll tell Miss Mayes you're bothering me."

"Go ahead and tell, tattletale," he would say, and of course they never did. But they wouldn't talk to him; they just kept on writing.

He would pull the girls' curls and knock the books off desks when he walked to the pencil sharpener. He would pronounce the word quickly if a reader paused to figure it out. He would call the right answer if the pupil hesitated an instant. He would stick out a foot to trip anyone who passed his desk.

VI-3 began to notice him all right, but it wasn't good. It was worse than being ignored.

One morning during recess the boys went into a huddle, and then Jack called Chris to join them.

Jack was the big boy who had answered Chris that first morning at school. He was one of the VI-3 leaders, Chris had learned, a big boy, tall as Chris but heavy-set instead of slender. The other leader was Tom. He was a small boy, all skinny arms and legs and big, loud mouth.

"It's the custom of the school," Jack told Chris, "for each new boy to run the gauntlet. So get ready."

"What's the gauntlet? How do you run it?" Chris asked. Now I'm making friends, he thought happily.

30

"It's a belt line, you dope," Jack answered, and Chris's heart dropped again.

"Line up, you guys," Tom shouted. "And you, Chris, get ready to run down the line!"

Chris faced the long line of boys with belts in hand ready to wallop him. He had run the belt line before and hated it. But he knew he must not falter. If he showed he was afraid, if he acted like a sissy who couldn't take it, he would never be admitted to the gang.

So he clenched his teeth and when Jack said, "Go!" he ran down the line of wildly beating belts without a murmur.

They can't call me a sissy, he thought proudly. Now I've passed their test! Maybe they'll be friends.

But he was wrong. Jack called the other boys into a huddle again. When they came out of it, "We forgot to tell you," Jack said. "A new guy has to run the gauntlet for each section of his grade. This afternoon you'll run for VI-1, tomorrow for VI-2 and VI-4."

"I don't believe it," said Chris. "You're just making that up."

"Listen to the fraidy cat," said Tom. The others took it up.

"Fraidy cat!"
"Can't take it!"
"Chicken!"

"I can too take it! I'll show you! I'll run your old gauntlet fifty times!"

But before he was halfway down the belt line that afternoon, Mr. Elson stopped them.

"What's the meaning of this?" he demanded.

"Nothing," half a dozen boys answered innocently. "We're just playing."

"Who started it?"

Nobody knew.

"Who else went down the line?"

"Nobody."

"Why Chris?"

Nobody knew — except Cotton, who never knew when to keep his mouth shut. "He's too smart. We have to take him down a peg or two."

"Well, I'm going to get to the bottom of this. Belt lines will not be tolerated. Chris, go into my office and wait for me."

So once again Chris sat in the small inner office, his heart thudding with fright.

Mr. Elson came in looking grave. He sat down, placed the tips of his fingers together, and looked at them thoughtfully.

"Chris," he asked, "what have you been doing to make the other boys angry?"

"I don't know, sir."

32

"Then why were they running you down the belt line?"

"It was just a game, sir."

"Who started this game?"

"I don't know, sir."

"You mean you won't tell me?"

"I can't tell you, sir."

"I could take that two ways. Oh, Miss Mayes, come in. One of your boys has gotten into difficulty "

"Yes, Mr. Elson," said Miss Mayes. She walked over to Chris and put her hand on his shoulder. "I've been questioning the other boys about it, and I feel sure that Chris is not intentionally to blame. I think the other boys are more to blame than he. It's a question of adjustment. I believe I can handle it if you'll let me."

"All right, Miss Mayes. Call on me if you need help. You understand, Chris, I'm not blaming you now. I'm just trying to get at the truth. You may go with Miss Mayes."

That was the first day VI-3 noticed Chris. Next day they thought up a game called Target. They unanimously chose Chris as the target, and the game consisted of peppering him with chinaberries shot from their rubber guns.

When they came in from recess, Miss Mayes noticed the red spots on Chris's face and arms.

"Why, Chris," she said, "come here and let me look at you. Are you coming down with measles?"

"No, ma'am," Chris said, standing before her stiff with embarrassment, feeling his face flush redder still.

Miss Mayes put a soft cool hand on his forehead. "Are you feverish? Does anything hurt you?"

"No, ma'am. I feel fine."

"Well, I can't understand those red spots. Perhaps you'd better go to the school nurse."

"No, ma'am. I'm all right," Chris objected.

Then Cotton, the blabber-mouth, spoke up. "You don't have to worry, Miss Mayes," he said. "Those are just chinaberry marks."

The whole class gave a disgusted sigh. The cat was out of the bag, and in a few moments Miss Mayes knew all about Target.

"All right, boys," she said, "march up to my desk single file and put your rubber guns and ammunition on my desk. You may get the guns after four o'clock, but remember — no more guns in school — no rubber guns, no cap pistols, no bean shooters, no sling shots. Have I covered the field?"

"How about water pistols?" asked Cotton.

"No water pistols," said Miss Mayes firmly.

So that ended the game of Target.

That night Chris overheard a conversation. Dad

was called to the telephone in the hall, and Chris couldn't help but listen.

"Oh, Miss Mayes," said Dad gayly. "Hello, there! That boy of mine been giving you any trouble? He'd better not, the young scamp, or he'll have to settle with me too."

There was a pause. Then Dad replied thoughtfully, "I see. I'm always out at the rig during school hours. Suppose I come to see you tonight. Maybe we can work something out together." 1545969

Another pause.

"Well, fine. I'll be there at 8:30. I'm very glad you called, Miss Mayes."

Dad came in and changed to his best slacks and new blue shirt. "I'm going to see your teacher," he said. "Anything you want me to tell her?"

"No, sir. I can't think of anything."

"Well, finish your homework before you start reading. And don't wait up for me. I may be late."

But Chris couldn't lose himself in his library book as usual. He couldn't go to sleep, either, for wondering what Dad and Miss Mayes were saying about him. He was still awake when Dad came in quietly, not turning on the light.

"Hi, Dad," said Chris, sitting up in bed.

"You still awake?" asked Dad. He came over and

35

sat on the bed beside Chris and put an arm around him. "Everything's going to be all right, Chris," he said. "It may take a little time, but everything will work out fine. Just remember this, Son, will you? That you won't get anywhere by talking loud and pushing people around."

"But I have to, Dad. If I don't, they act like I'm not there. They make me feel like a ghost, a lonesome black ghost!"

"A black ghost?" teased Dad. "Now, really, Chris! But seriously, Son. You can't expect to have a whole roomful of friends. You can expect to have one or two. And the way to get them is not by being a loud-mouthed show-off, ready to fight at the drop of a hat."

"Then what is the way, Dad?"

Dad laughed a little and hugged him close for an instant. "That's a hard one to answer, Chris," he said. "All I can say is just by being the nicest person you know how to be. That'll get results, I bet you!"

4

Saturday at the Rig

Chris didn't complain to Dad about going to school after the very first. He knew it would be useless. Besides he did not want to be a whiner. But every morning when he woke up, he felt the same sick dread of school that he had felt that first day. Only now his fears were based on realities, not imaginings.

He didn't know how he could have stood it if he hadn't had Saturdays at the rig with Dad to look forward to. Then he forgot all about school and its problems, for each Saturday the world was a new and wonderful place.

He didn't even mind getting up at five o'clock, for he enjoyed the long drive through the country while the new day dawned; and when they got to the rig, it was fun to watch the crew at work on the well or to explore the farm or ranch where they were drilling.

It was most fun in fall and spring. In fall Dad nearly always got permission to hunt doves and quail in season. Chris enjoyed hunting and was a good shot. Birds had been scarce for the last few years because of the long drought, but Chris often shot enough for a meal. Sometimes, with Dad's help, he would cook a bird stew out at the rig, and he thought nothing in the world tasted so good.

But all in all, spring was his favorite time to spend at the rig. Now, in April, the country was at its best. All the bare trees had sprouted out, and the live oaks had put on a fresh coat of tender green. There had been enough rain to make the grass green too, and to bring out wild flowers by the thousands. The cattle had been kept out of the pasture where the men were drilling, and it was spread with a gay carpet of red phlox and firewheels and white and yellow daisies.

Chris hunted rabbits in the spring, and squirrels, too. There was a creek bordered by tall trees in this pasture, an ideal place to look for squirrels.

Of course it was still dark when they arrived at the rig. The tall derrick strung with lights always gave Chris a thrill of excitement. He would sit in the warm car and

38

watch the men from the new tour, or shift, take over the work of the men on the night tour. As they moved back and forth between the darkness and light they looked like tiny mechanical men in comparison with the huge machinery with which they worked.

One Saturday, when it was barely daylight, Chris took his gun and headed for the trees along the creek to hunt squirrels. He shivered a little as he walked through the wild flowers, partly from the before-sunrise chill, partly from the sense of excitement he always felt when he went hunting.

He stepped into the woods cautiously, but the dry leaves of winter were still thick on the ground and crackled under his feet. He took half a dozen tiptoe steps and stood still. He loaded and pumped his gun and waited, peering keenly upward into the leafy branches overhead.

At first he could see nothing among the leaves, not even the birds busy at their joyful morning twittering. Then gradually, as the daylight grew brighter, he could make out the birds as they flitted from limb to limb. He even saw two nests.

After a long time he saw a squirrel like a moving bump on one of the branches. He raised his gun to his shoulder, but before he could aim, the squirrel was out of sight. He stood still as a post, and presently the squirrel ran out on the branch again.

"I'll wait till I can get a real good shot," Chris decided. "One shot is all I'll get. As soon as my gun goes off, I won't see hide or hair of a squirrel any more this morning."

As he watched, perfectly quiet, he saw a second squirrel run out after the first, and then another and another till he counted five. Motionless, forgetting to aim, he watched the squirrels frisk about like children playing hide and seek. Sometimes their tails would be stiffly erect, sometimes waving straight behind. They raced up one limb and down another and leaped from one tree to another so far away they seemed to be flying.

For a good twenty minutes Chris watched the squirrels. Then from out of nowhere a helicopter appeared. It dipped low over the creek with a buzz and a whine. For an instant there was a flurry of wildly waving tails; then the squirrels disappeared from sight. Nothing moved on the branch. A bit of bark fluttered earthward.

"Missed 'em," muttered Chris. "A perfect setup like that, and I didn't fire a shot!"

But he wasn't really sorry. He had never before seen so many squirrels frisking together, and they had looked so carefree and funny. He wanted a squirrel skin to tan, but after all, where could he keep it through the smelly period, at Mrs. Whittset's?

He sneaked over to another clump of trees and waited and watched for a long time, but he didn't see another squirrel. At last he decided to hunt a rabbit for Lem's dog. Lem was the toolpusher on the job, and he always had his collie with him.

When he walked out into the pasture he saw a rabbit leaping through the flowers almost at once, but it was much too far away to shoot. But that showed there were rabbits around here, thought Chris, running toward the place where the rabbit had disappeared. Then he began stalking through the grass and flowers, near clumps of agarita, chaparral, and cactus, hoping to scare a rabbit up ahead of him. He wandered far away from the rig. But he couldn't get lost, because the tall derrick would always guide him back.

The sun was hot on his back and he was almost ready to quit before he jumped his rabbit. But it was close enough so that he could draw a good bead on it. He fired, and the cottontail rabbit fell, shot through the head. He picked it up and started back to the rig.

When he got there, he shed his coat, threw the rabbit to Lem's dog, and went to the car for his fishing tackle. Dad had bought him a new fly rod because he never had a place to dig fishing worms. Now he wanted to practice casting, always with the hope that he would hook a big fish.

Dad saw him heading toward the creek. "Hey, Chris," he called, "look for a good swimming hole! It's sure hot enough for a good swim today. How about taking one during my noon hour?"

"Okay," Chris called back.

For the next hour and a half, Chris wandered along the creek. Where the underbrush allowed him to swing freely, he practiced casting, changing his fly several times at each likely pool. He didn't catch anything, but he had three good strikes, all of them on his Silver Doctor. And his casting was improving. He had to untangle only two bad backlashes.

As he fished, he looked for a good swimming hole. When he saw a promising pool, he tested it by chunking rocks in to see whether it was deep enough. He found a good one, too, not very far from the rig. When he could tell by the shadows that it was nearly noon, he left the creek bank and walked through the trees to the open pasture. There he waited until he saw his father get off work for lunch. Then he whistled and waved and beckoned till his father spotted him and waved back.

Lem and his dog came too, and all of them had a good swim. The water was cool, but the day was so hot, even for a Texas April, that it felt fine.

The men had brought their lunches, and after their swim they had a picnic under the trees. Dad had provided ham sandwiches and hardboiled eggs, pickles, and apples, and Lem's wife had put in so many homemade cookies that he divided with them. There was a thermos with coffee for each of the men and a quart bottle of milk for Chris.

After lunch the men went back to the job and Chris stayed at the creek and fished.

Once when he stepped over a rotting log, he saw a small gray snake wriggle under it. "I wish I could catch that snake," he said to himself. "I could take it to school and maybe trade it to one of the boys for a knife or some marbles. Or at least I could have fun scaring the girls. But what could I put it in?"

He remembered the almost empty milk bottle and ran back to where they had left the lunch kit. He hurriedly drank some more of the milk and poured the rest out, carefully saving the bottle cap. Then he cut two sticks, one straight and one with a small fork at the end.

Back at the log, with sticks and bottle ready, he kicked the log over. Under it was not one but at least half a dozen small snakes.

Chris worked carefully but swiftly, picking up the wriggling little snakes with his sticks and trying to put them into the bottle. Time after time they slithered away or slipped out of his sticks just before he could drop them in. At last he got one snake into the bottle. Then his work was doubled, for he had to keep it from getting out while he tried to put another in. Finally he succeeded in capturing three of the snakes before the others got away. He put the cap firmly on the bottle, cut a few slits in it for air, put the bottle with the lunch kit, and went back to fishing.

But it wasn't his day for catching fish. By the middle of the afternoon he had nothing to show for all his efforts but an arm that was beginning to ache. "It's just too hot for fish to bite," he decided. He walked back to the rig, lunch kit under one arm, fly rod and bottle of snakes under the other.

At a safe distance he sat down in the shade of a mesquite tree and watched the men work. Overhead a mockingbird sang, undaunted either by his presence or the noise of the drilling.

His eyes took in the neat, familiar pattern of the rig. Off to one side was the long shed painted bright blue where tools and equipment were stored. Between the shed and the derrick was the pile of big, long pipes stacked above ground on steel supports. Off to the other side was the small office that was Dad's headquarters. Just beyond was the slush pit, from which mud was pumped down into the well to cool the drill, which otherwise would get too hot from friction.

The main center of interest was the derrick itself,

rising above a platform as high as the second story of an old house. This platform and the walls below were painted the same cheerful blue as the shed, with the railings and danger spots in bright red. At one side were the gas engines that powered the drilling, and the tower rose from the other side, seventy-five feet high. It was a jackknife rig, which meant that to move it, it was not necessary to tear it down completely. It folded like a giant jackknife, so that it could be carried away on a huge truck.

The rig looked delicate and lacy and silvery in the bright sunlight, with the bracings and ladder that went all the way to the top making patterns against the sky. But it was really strong and massive steel.

There was not much action to watch. Four or five men moved about — aimlessly, it seemed, but Chris knew that each of them was doing his job: checking the steam pressure, looking at the whirling drill stem, throwing the switch that started or stopped the machinery.

The huge traveling block that carried the drill was low down on the rig. The drill stem whirled, and the traveling block moved downward so slowly that Chris could not tell it moved at all except by sighting it against one of the braces on the tower.

Finally the drill had gone as far as it could. One of the men stopped the drilling and sent the traveling block upwards. Two others were waiting with giant pliers to swing the drill aside and attach a new length of drill stem. They worked easily, almost lazily. Yet Chris knew that every movement was timed to the second, that any undue delay or speed could mean disaster.

The whole operation took less than ten minutes. Then the traveling block was sent to the top of the derrick again, and the drill stem began to whirl once more as it bored ever deeper into the earth.

This was what drilling for oil meant. This process was repeated over and over, day and night, from the time that casing was set on the well to the time that the well was brought in, either as an oil well or as a gasser, or was abandoned. Sometimes, of course, there was a breakdown in the machinery or the drill slipped loose and was lost in the hole and the workers had to "go fishing" for it.

Chris wanted to be a driller like Dad when he grew up. He would have to start as a roughneck, he realized, and work up to be a toolpusher before he could be a driller. Dad wanted him to go to college and become a geological engineer, but he thought he'd rather be a driller.

He sat and watched the traveling block move slowly downward, sending the whirling drill stem deeper by the minute. The whirling and the rhythmical hum of the motors made him drowsy. Soon he was sprawling in the grass, and before he knew it, he was dozing.

The buzz of a helicopter woke him.

All day he had heard the whine and buzz of helicopters flying low over the pasture. When Dad got off work and they walked toward the car, Chris couldn't wait to find out about them. "Dad, have you noticed all these helicopters?" he asked.

"Looks like a lot of them, but it's really only one, flying back and forth half a dozen times a day."

"What's it doing way out here?"

"Guess."

"Oh, Dad, I can't! I've been trying to figure it out all day. Tell me!"

"It's prospecting for uranium."

"Oh, Dad, quit teasing and tell me!"

"I am telling you. It's prospecting for uranium."

"How on earth could it do that?"

"With a scintillator."

"What's a scintillator?"

"It's a little machine with a Geiger counter. When the helicopter flies low enough over uranium deposits, the scintillator registers it."

"Have they found any uranium here?"

"I don't know. Most of the oil companies are checking their leases, but they're keeping mighty quiet about

47

what they find. It is known, however, that a rich uranium field has been found in Karnes County."

"Where's Karnes County?"

"Right next to this one."

"Oh. Do you think they'll find any here?"

"I don't know. Geologists say it isn't likely. The rock formation isn't right. What have you got in the milk bottle?"

"Snakes. Look."

Dad looked. Then he grabbed the bottle.

"Chris, for the love of Pete!" he exclaimed. "You scare the living daylights out of me!"

"What's the matter, Dad?"

"Don't you know what these are? They're rattle-snakes! I can see I'm going to have to educate you about the poisonous snakes of Texas, my son!"

"I know they're rattlesnakes, Dad. I was careful."

"What in the world do you think you're going to do with live rattlesnakes?"

"Take them to school and show them to the kids. I bet a lot of them have never even seen a rattlesnake."

"No, you're not," said Dad firmly.

"But why not? Don't you think they'd think I was sort of brave to catch them?"

"They'd probably think you were sort of crazy, especially Miss Mayes."

"Oh, Dad, I won't let them bite anyone!"

"You couldn't be sure. No, Chris. Never play with danger."

"But, Dad, I thought — "

"Believe me, Chris, these rattlesnakes won't help you to win friends and influence people. We're going to get rid of them here and now. And next time you see a rattlesnake I want you to do one of two things. Either kill it or go in the other direction fast!"

5

The Dumb Oily Orphan

The next Monday the kids began calling Chris names. They called him "Oily" because his father worked on an oil rig. Then they learned that his mother was dead, and that led to "Oily Orphan." One day he let it slip that he was repeating the sixth grade, and from then on he was the "Dumb Oily Orphan."

It made him furious. They could have called him "Jewel" or "President" or "Dearest" and it would have made him equally furious, because he knew that whatever words they chose, they intended to hurt him.

Friday one of the girls thought up a new game in geography study period. She printed "Dumb Oily

Orphan" on a sheet of notebook paper. Then she found a picture of a wild-looking native of Africa in her geography, put the sign under the picture, and held the book up for all to see. Others took up the game with silent glee.

In one part of the room after another the sign sprang up under a strange ugly picture of an ape, a water buffalo, a starving native, a boa constrictor. While Miss Mayes wrote questions on the board, VI-3 noiselessly chuckled at each other's wit, fiendishly pleased at being able to hurt Chris.

And they did hurt him. From his seat in the back of the room he could see all the pictures. He pretended not to look, but he saw them all the same, and he could feel his face burning with shame and anger.

Tom, the boy next to him, prodded him and pointed to a particularly vicious picture.

"I don't care," Chris muttered. "You're nothing but a bunch of local yokels!"

Tom reached over and hit Chris in the face.

Miss Mayes turned around just in time to see.

"Tom," she said sharply, "come here instantly!"

"It's his fault," Tom said. "He called us bad names."

"Did you call him a bad name, Chris?"

"No, ma'am."

"He did too, Miss Mayes!"

51

"Oh, I did not! All I said was that you're a bunch of local yokels."

"See, he said it again!"

"Why did you call them local yokels, Chris?"

"Because that's what my dad calls them when he means they're not important."

"I see. And had Tom called you a name?"

"Well, no, ma'am. Not exactly."

"Then why did you call him a name?"

"I — I just felt like it."

Anne had forgotten her sign and left it face up on her desk. Miss Mayes saw it and realized what had been happening. "Well, both you boys owe me an apology for disturbing the class when my back was turned," she said.

"I'm sorry, Miss Mayes. I won't do it again," said both boys quickly.

"And each of you owes an apology to the other."

"Aw, Miss Mayes!"

"All right, if you're not in the right spirit to apologize, we'll just wait. Both of you report to me when school is out. Now our geography period is gone, and it's time to start spelling. But first I want to send a note to Mrs. Adkins." She wrote quickly, put the note in an envelope, and sealed it. "Chris, will you take this note for me? You won't have any trouble finding Mrs. Adkins.

She's in the very last room in the west corridor."

Chris jumped up quickly. "Yes, ma'am," he said. He felt better to know that Miss Mayes wasn't angry at him.

He didn't have to go all the long way down the west corridor. When he went into the hall, he saw Mrs. Adkins just leaving the teachers' lounge. He hurried and caught up with her, delivered the note, and went back to VI-3, proud to complete his mission so quickly.

But before he reached the door, he heard his name through the transom, and he stopped to listen.

Miss Mayes was speaking. Her voice sounded very sad.

"I am very much disappointed in you, boys and girls," she was saying, "disappointed and ashamed.

"I want you to think for a moment, each one of you, how you would feel if tomorrow you had to leave Oakdale and start school in a strange town where you knew no one. How would you feel if your classmates were unkind? If they ignored you and taunted you and hurt you?

"Boys and girls, this is your problem, to make Chris feel welcome and happy among you. I thought that you could solve it, that you were friendly enough and generous enough to do it. Was I mistaken?

"I have not said anything before, but I have seen

how you treated Chris. Chris is not perfect. He has done things to make you angry. But, you boys, haven't you noticed that he has kept you out of trouble? It would have been easy for him to have named names to Mr. Elson or to me, but he's no tattletale. It would have been easy for him to have whimpered or complained when you ran him through the belt line or shot him with chinaberries. Boys and girls, Chris Gregory's a brave boy, the kind you should be proud to have for a friend.

"He'll be coming back any minute now, and I don't want him to know anything about what I've said. But, boys and girls, am I going to have to be ashamed of my class?"

VI-3 was so still you could have heard a pin drop.

"Open your spellers at page 72," said Miss Mayes, and a rustling sound went over the room.

Outside in the corridor, Chris felt tears running down his cheeks. He wiped them away impatiently with the back of his hand. He didn't care what the kids did now. Miss Mayes had said he was a brave boy, the kind you wanted for a friend!

He walked into the room, head high, smiling proudly. "I delivered your note, Miss Mayes," he said.

"Thank you, Chris," Miss Mayes replied. "We're studying our spelling now."

When he was seated, Cotton raised his hand.

"May I speak to Chris?" he asked.

"You may," said Miss Mayes, smiling.

Cotton went over and squeezed into the seat with Chris. "Our spelling is on page 72," he whispered.

Monday morning when Chris reached school he saw a crowd of boys and girls clustered together.

Chris pushed his way in and found everybody gathered around a boy he hadn't seen before. "Another new boy?" he asked Cotton, who happened to be standing next to him.

"No," answered Cotton. "Not a new boy. He's a VI-3'er who's been out of school sick for almost a month."

"Who is he?"

"Freddie Felsing. He's keen! He lives in the country and comes in on the bus."

Chris sized the boy up. He was not quite as tall as Chris, stockily built, curly-haired and blue-eyed, rosy and plump in spite of having been sick. He sat on the steps, and it was like a king receiving homage from his people. Each new arrival at school came up for a few minutes at least. Freddie answered their greetings with joking remarks, and the boys and girls responded to everything he said with appreciative laughter.

With a sinking heart Chris realized that the actual leader of VI-3 was not Jack and it was not Tom. It was

Freddie Felsing. What new torments would he think of? Freddie's first contact with Chris came that morning in arithmetic class. Miss Mayes was sitting with Ruthie, helping her with her decimal points. Chris looked up from his problem just in time to see Tom dip Betsy's pigtail in his bottle of ink. Betsy, feeling Tom's touch, reached back and tossed her braids over her shoulder. As she did so, ink from the dipped pigtail flipped across Tom's nose. The funniest expression of surprise and embarrassment wrinkled Tom's face. Chris couldn't help laughing to himself. Just then he caught the eye of Freddie, who had watched the incident also, and the two smiled together as if they were friends.

"I could like Freddie," Chris decided.

He couldn't help thinking about Miss Mayes's appeal to VI-3 Friday, and about Freddie, who hadn't heard it. In several small ways he could tell that the boys and girls of the class had listened to her, and he accepted their little efforts toward friendship gratefully. One boy offered to let him have his library book next. One of the captains of the spelling match chose him right after the best spellers, so that he stood in the middle of the line instead of at the foot. And at recess, they let him be third baseman.

But he kept wondering when he'd have to have a showdown with Freddie.

At lunch period, as usual, everyone raced and pushed to be first in line at the cafeteria. When places in line had been established, the boys began calling, "Hey, Freddie, come sit by me!" "I'm saving a place for you, Freddie!" "Here's a place with me, Freddie!"

Freddie sauntered down the line with a smile and a pat on the back for these friends, but he didn't stop until he reached Chris at the end of the line. "Thanks, kids," he called, "but I want to sit here today."

He took his place behind Chris. "What's he planning to do to me?" Chris wondered, so nervous he almost spilled his milk. "Maybe he won't sit next to me after all."

But Freddie did sit next to him. "You're Oily, aren't you?" he began at once.

"That's not my name," answered Chris, wary as a cat seeing a dog approach.

"Aw, everybody's got to have a nickname," Freddie said easily. "I've got half a dozen. Fried-Eye, Giggles, Cherry, or Curly. And at home I'm Sonny. But generally I'm just plain Freddie. Just take your pick. I'll answer to any one of 'em."

"Cherry is because he likes cherries so much," Cotton explained from across the table. "I like them too."

Chris sat silent, eating without tasting his food.

"I've been hearing about you, Oily," Freddie said.

57

Here it comes! thought Chris. "You have?" he answered carefully.

"Sure have. Heard you were a keen ball player."

"You did?" Chris said.

"Yes," said Freddie. "That's what I heard. So how about playing left field on my team at P. E. today?"

What does this mean? Chris wondered. He tried to think what to say. But before he could answer, boys within earshot began clamoring. "Hey, Freddie, let me be your first baseman!"

"Say, Curly, can I be on your team too?"

"Let me play on your side, Freddie."

Freddie brushed them aside.

"Well," he asked, "what about it? Are you going to be on my team?"

In a sudden glad rush Chris realized that Freddie really wanted him, that he was not an enemy but a friend.

"Yes," he answered eagerly. "I sure will!"

In the game that afternoon Chris was so anxious to make good that he was nervous and tense. He fumbled the very first ball that came his way.

"That's all right, kid," called Freddie. Chris steadied down then and did all right.

In the last inning, with Freddie's team only one run ahead, their opponents had the tying run on third, the winning run on second, and two men out. The batter hit a long, long fly that looked like a homer for sure. But Chris raced away back and caught it against the fence for the final out.

"Hey, Oily, that's all right!" Freddie's voice rang out.

Chris tried to look modest, but he couldn't, because he was grinning from ear to ear with happiness.

That evening when Dad came in with the groceries, the kitchen table was piled high with Chris's books.

"Chris," Dad called, standing with the big sack in his arms, "come and get your books off the table." He sounded cross.

Chris hurried to clear the table. He shoveled the books on to the nearest chair.

"For the love of Pete, Chris," Dad said, setting the heavy bag on the table, "why do you let your library books accumulate like this? You must owe a fortune in library fines. Don't come to me for money to pay them. It'll have to come out of your allowance. You'll simply have to learn to be punctual."

"These books aren't overdue," said Chris. "I just got them today."

"All these books?"

"Some of them are my textbooks."

"But there must be half a dozen library books."

"Seven."

"For the love of Pete, why do you check out so many at one time?"

"We can go to the library to check out books just once a week. I have to get enough to last me until the next library period."

Dad began to pick up the books and read the titles. "*King of the Wind, All about the Wonders of Chemistry, Boy's Book of Rockets, Wilderness Pioneer, Caves of the Great Hunters, Haunt Fox.* Do you mean to tell me you read a book a day? Big books like these?"

"Sure."

"Do you mean that as soon as you come home from school you sit down and start reading?"

"Well, not exactly."

"What do you mean, not exactly?"

"Well, generally I lie down."

"But you spend all afternoon reading?"

"Sure, most of the time."

"Why?"

"Well, what else is there to do?"

"Why don't you play with some of the boys in your school?"

"Nobody to play with."

"You mean nobody comes to see you? You don't go to see anybody?"

60

"No, sir," said Chris, miserably.

"Why, Chris?"

"I don't know why. The kids just don't like me."

"But there must be a reason."

"I guess they just don't like a new kid butting in to their gangs. They have everything settled. They don't want it interrupted."

"Why don't you join one of the gangs?"

"Dad," said Chris desperately, "you don't ask them to let you join. They have to ask you."

Dad heard the desperation in Chris's voice. "I'm not trying to badger you, Chris," he said. "I'm just trying to find out. It's not good for a boy your age to sit in the house all day. You ought to be outdoors playing, getting exercise in the fresh air. You oughtn't sit in the house reading every afternoon."

"I like to read now, Dad. It's fun. When I'm reading I forget about everything else."

Dad clamped his jaws together so that the muscles in his cheeks bulged out. "I see," he said evenly.

"Besides, sometimes I work on my model planes."

"But you ought to be out in the fresh air. Tell you what. Until you find a friend, you and I will just have to do things together. Next time I play golf, how about caddying for me? That way you can make a little extra money, too."

"Okay," Chris agreed without enthusiasm. "But I've got a friend now. At least I think I have. I like him, and I think he likes me."

"That's fine. Invite him over."

"He couldn't come. He lives in the country."

"Who is he? A new kid like you?"

"No, he's been sick. His name is Freddie Felsing. He's swell. Everybody in the class likes him."

"That kind, is he? Well, you'd better not set your heart on having him for a friend if he's got so many already. That's the hardest kind to get. Better look for a kid that seems a little left out too. He'll be looking for a friend and will be glad to meet you more than half way."

"But I like Freddie. You've got to like your friend. You've got to like him right off! You can't just say, 'I want a friend, and he wants a friend, so we'll be friends of each other's.' It's — it's sort of a magic feeling when you're friends."

"Well, Chris, you may be right at that. Friendship is a sort of magic feeling."

6

More Trouble

A few evenings later when Dad came in, he said, "Chris, I heard at the rig today that the swimming pool in Cuero is open. Think it's warm enough for us to drive over for a swim after supper?"

"Oh, sure, Dad. That will be swell. Let's not cook supper. Let's just get hamburgers and go on."

Dad laughed. "Okay," he agreed. "Suits me."

The pool, with the lights sparkling on the water and the swimmers laughing and shouting, was pleasantly exciting. There were enough hardy souls who had braved the spring chill to make it fun. One of these was Miss Mayes.

Dad saw her first. "Why, there's your pretty teacher," he said as he and Chris stood for a minute looking over the pool.

Miss Mayes, in a coral colored bathing suit, was walking out on the diving board. Chris and Dad watched her dive gracefully, but Chris was more interested in the boys playing water polo with a red ball. He did not know any of them, but he made a running dive from the edge of the pool and swam toward them.

When he hit the water, it was so cold it made him gasp. But he began to swim vigorously and soon felt warm and comfortable. The boys with the ball paid no attention to him. He swam the length of the pool twice, dodging the boys and their game. As he passed them the third time, one of the boys called, "Hey, want to get in the game with us? We need another kid to make the sides even, and you look like you swim good enough."

"Sure," said Chris. "Whose side am I on?"

They had a great time swimming and splashing and dodging and laughing breathlessly till one of the mothers called firmly, "Time to go home now, Cliff," and broke up the game.

Alone again, Chris stood in water up to his chin and looked around the pool. On the rim of the pool over at the deep end Dad and Miss Mayes sat laughing together, Miss Mayes wrapped in a big beach towel. On her other

64

side a man sat glumly, pulling up blades of grass and tossing them into the water.

"That must be her date," Chris thought. "I'll bet he's burned up about Dad."

He looked across the pool. Sitting by himself with his legs dangling in the water was Jack. Chris was glad to see a boy he knew in the crowd. Without stopping to think how Jack might greet him, he swam over to him under water and bobbed up at his feet.

"Hi, Jack," he said cordially.

Jack looked at him without answering. As Chris reached for the rail, Jack put a foot on each of his shoulders and pushed him down hard.

Chris did not mind the sudden vicious ducking. But when he tried to come up, Jack's feet still held him down. He went deeper till the feet no longer touched him and came up sputtering, out of Jack's reach.

"What's the big idea?" he called. "You didn't have to be that rough!"

"I guess that'll teach you," Jack taunted. "Just leave me alone."

The old hurt flared in Chris, but he was angry, too. He swam to the edge of the pool, climbed out, and ran behind Jack. "Turn about's fair play," he said and pushed him into the water.

Jack came up sputtering and thrashing. "Help!" he

65

gasped. "I can't swim!"

Chris jumped in after him, caught him, and pulled him to the surface. He tried to tow him to the rail, but Jack was panicky. He grabbed Chris around the neck, and down they went together.

Chris fought his way to the surface, Jack still clinging chokingly. "Dad!" he shouted.

He had just time to see Dad come to his feet and dive before Jack pulled him under again.

In a minute Dad reached them, and almost at the same time, the life guard. Dad grabbed Chris, and the guard broke Jack's hold. The men pulled both boys out of the water.

Both boys were coughing and sputtering, Jack more than Chris, for Chris was used to swimming under water. All the other swimmers crowded around them as they fought for breath.

"What happened?" asked Dad when Chris could talk.

"I pushed Jack in," Chris explained. "I didn't know he couldn't swim."

"You should be more careful," Dad warned. "Next time you push a kid in, be sure he can swim."

"Yes, sir," said Chris. "I'm sorry, Jack."

"Let me alone," muttered Jack.

"Is that all you can say?" asked the guard. "The kid

shouldn't have pushed you in, but he did try to save your life — may have done it. Seems to me you could show a little gratitude!"

"Forget it," said Dad. "Come on, Chris. Let's go home."

Next day in school Chris felt again the old dislike. VI-3 was cold and hard against him. Even Freddie acted troubled and embarrassed and barely spoke to him.

The room buzzed with whispers about the near drowning in the swimming pool. By afternoon recess Nell could stand it no longer. "Miss Mayes," she said, shocked, "do you know that last night Chris tried to drown Jack? Isn't it awful to have a boy like that in our room?"

"Nonsense," said Miss Mayes firmly. "Chris didn't try to drown anyone. Is that what the class has been fluttering about all day? We'll soon fix that!"

As soon as everyone was seated after recess, Miss Mayes said, "Class, it has been brought to my attention that some of you think Chris tried to drown Jack last night. That is a terrible accusation, and it is utterly untrue. I know, because I happened to be at the pool last night.

"I don't know how this tale got started, but I'm going to let you hear the truth from the boys themselves.

Chris and Jack, will you please come forward?"

Chris stumbled to his feet and walked up the aisle. He felt sick with unhappiness, but he held his head high. His eyes burned, and he was afraid he was going to cry. He bit the inside of his cheeks, and the pain helped him to control himself. Jack came and stood beside him, his hands in his pockets, looking at the floor.

"Now, Jack," asked Miss Mayes, "did Chris try to drown you?"

"He pushed me in water over my head, and I can't swim," Jack blustered.

"Chris, did you know Jack can't swim?" Miss Mayes asked.

"No, ma'am," Chris answered.

"Jack, did Chris know you can't swim?"

"No, ma'am, I guess not," Jack admitted sullenly.

"So that when he pushed you in, Chris had no intention of drowning you. Chris, did you actually push Jack in?"

"Yes, ma'am."

"Why?"

"Because he ducked me, and I thought turn about was fair play."

"Jack, did you duck Chris first?"

"Yes, ma'am."

"So that it was not unusual for Chris to push you in.

Probably any boy in the room would have done the same thing. Now when you were pushed into the water, what did you do, Jack?"

"I yelled for help. I yelled that I couldn't swim."

"What did you do then, Chris?"

"I jumped in to pull him out."

A long excited sigh swept the room.

"Did you pull him out?"

"No, ma'am. I tried to, but I couldn't."

"Why not?"

"Jack grabbed me around the neck and kept pulling me under."

"Jack, did you grab Chris around the neck?"

"Yes, ma'am. I guess I did. I had to grab something to keep from sinking."

"Then what happened?"

"Dad and the lifeguard came and pulled us out."

"So, class, if anybody almost drowned anybody, it was really Jack who almost drowned Chris by getting a strangle hold on his neck. But nobody would be foolish enough to accuse Jack of trying to drown Chris. What Jack did in grabbing Chris was perfectly natural. It was the wrong thing to do, but it's what most people do when they get panicky in the water.

"You boys may be seated," said Miss Mayes. "Now there are three things I want every one of you to learn

69

from this experience. The first one is the evil of gossip and the harm it can do. The second one is the rules of safety and good manners at the swimming pool. And the third one is what to do to prevent a drowning. I want you to think about the first one. The other two we'll study in health today instead of our regular lesson. We'll find out what to do if someone gets a strangle hold on you in the water and how to try to rescue a drowning person. Now I'm going to the library to get some books on swimming and safety for us to use as references, and while I'm gone, I don't want to hear a peep out of any of you."

She went out, leaving the door open. The class sat silently for a moment, listening to the click of her heels down the corridor. Then "Peep!" said Cotton in a tiny voice.

A soft wave of laughter rippled over the room, and everyone felt better.

Freddie came over and sat with Chris. "I sure am dumb to think that you might do a thing like that," he apologized. "I ought to have my head examined!"

The class felt sorry for their unkindness too and wanted to make it up to Chris. Freddie gave them the opportunity the last period that afternoon in English Club.

"I nominate Chris for treasurer," he said.

Mary Belle, who liked Freddie, quickly seconded

the nomination. Jack nominated a girl, but when the votes were counted, Chris won, 22 to 13.

His election almost made Chris forget how miserable he had felt all day. He was very busy recording dues in the treasurer's book that Ann passed on to him, and very careful not to make a single mistake.

Once he looked up and found Miss Mayes smiling at him. Shyly he smiled back.

Next day when the bell ended their baseball game in P.E., Freddie walked back to the building with his arm across Chris's shoulder. Tom and Cotton were at his side and Pedro trailed behind. "Say, fellows," he said, "we looked pretty ragged today. How about you four guys getting together after school to practice?"

"Sure, Freddie," Tom answered.

"We can play in the vacant lot back of our house," Cotton said, "if we clean off the weeds."

"Well, this Saturday all of you get out there with hoes and clean the place up," Freddie ordered. "Then you'll be ready to start practicing Monday. It'll work out fine. Pedro is a pitcher, Tom a catcher, and Chris and Cotton fielders. You'll get pitching, catching, batting, and fielding practice. That certainly ought to give us the edge on Jack's team. Sure wish I could stay in town after school and practice with you!"

71

"Maybe you can," said Cotton, "some day when your mother has to come to town in the afternoon."

"Well, I'm sure going to try," Freddie promised.

"You guys be at my house at nine o'clock Saturday morning," Cotton told them. "Bring your own hoes."

Chris didn't hesitate to give up his Saturday at the rig. He was at Cotton's promptly, with the hoe he had bought with an advance on his allowance. Pedro was ahead of him, and Tom came in a few minutes. Soon they were hard at work, shirts off, sweating in the hot April sunshine. By noon they had all the weeds cut and raked into a big pile to dry and burn. They were sunburned and tired but very well pleased with themselves. Cotton's mother was so glad to have the lot cleaned that she treated them all to the movie that afternoon.

Beginning Monday, the boys met for practice every day after school. Often other boys joined them, and several times Freddie managed to stay in town and play with them. It was lots of fun, and their practice brought good results, too. Each day at school their game went a little smoother, with batting averages climbing up and errors getting fewer.

Chris didn't need an alarm clock to get him to school on time these days. He always woke up eager to be one of the first at school so he'd have time to play ball before the bell rang.

72

Things were going better in school in every way. The class didn't torment him any more, and they didn't ignore him. More and more they accepted him and included him in their work and games. Chris really was a good fielder. The other boys were beginning to recognize his skill and respect him for it.

His lessons were going better too. Miss Mayes had found out he'd skipped decimal fractions last year and this year both, because of moving, and she made him stay after school so that she could explain them to him and help him with his nouns and verbs. At first Chris almost hated her for making him miss practice, but when he found out how much easier arithmetic and language had become, he forgave her and was grateful.

Chris went home from practice each evening with a huge appetite for supper. Dad said he might just as well be feeding a pet anaconda. And after supper he was so sleepy that he could barely do his homework. He was ready for bed without a library book or a radio program first. He didn't even miss Dad when he went out oftener than usual in the evenings, and he would have been surprised to know that most of these times Dad was with Miss Mayes.

But he was never too tired when Dad suggested that they go swimming. Once he got enough courage to invite Cotton to go with them, and when Cotton accepted, he began asking some of the other boys too.

One Friday Freddie spent the night with him. They played ball after school, went swimming that night, and spent Saturday at the rig with Dad. Freddie was fascinated by the drilling operations. They had such a good time and Chris was so happy that he felt himself bubbling over with silliness.

School was swell.

Life in Oakdale was super.

And all because Freddie was his friend.

Chris began to think of this friendship as something precious that he owned, something all the dearer because any moment he might lose it.

For he knew that work on the oil well was progressing steadily. Soon it would be finished. When it was, he might have to move again, and all his bright new happiness would be lost.

7

Baby Sitter for Chris

One evening when he came in, Chris heard his father at the telephone.

"Fine, Margaret," Dad was saying. "I'll see you at eight, then."

"Dad," Chris said as his father came into the kitchen, "why didn't you let me know you were going to see Miss Mayes? I could have saved you the trouble."

"Believe me, Chris, it's no trouble," said Dad, smiling as he tied a towel around his waist for an apron. "Sizzling steaks tonight!"

"But, really, Dad, you don't have to go to see Miss Mayes. I'm getting along all right at school now. I'm getting along fine with the kids and in class too."

"I'm glad to hear that," Dad said, sprinkling salt on the griddle.

"Yes. I like school now. I really do. I wish we could stay here always."

"That's fine, Chris."

"So you see you don't have to talk to Miss Mayes about me any more."

"I wasn't planning to talk to her about you."

"You weren't?"

"Oh, of course we'll talk about you as my son, but not as a problem. I'm going to see Miss Mayes because I like her as a person."

"You mean you're having a date with her?"

"That's what I mean," Dad answered, slapping the steaks on the sizzling griddle. "Better start setting the table."

"But, Dad, a date with my schoolteacher!"

"Why not? Get out the lettuce and tomatoes when you finish the table. This won't take long."

"Well, I don't know," said Chris, carefully lining up plate, knife, and fork.

"One of the prettiest girls in Texas. Don't you like her? Isn't she a nice person?"

Chris took time to think before he answered. He remembered how she hadn't jumped down his throat the day he whistled at her, the way she took up for him in the principal's office, the time she stayed after school to help him with his arithmetic, the way she smiled at him — the way she had talked to the class about him that day.

"Yes," he said slowly, "I like her. She's a swell person!"

Dad had almost let the steaks burn waiting for Chris's answer. The two looked into each other's eyes, and both began to smile.

"Well, there you have it," said Dad.

A few nights later Chris woke up feeling sick.

"Dad," he called. "Dad!"

"Huh?" Dad answered sleepily. "What's the matter?"

"I feel sick. And I'm so hot." He threw off the covers as Dad got up and came over to him.

Dad put a hand on his forehead. It felt cold, and Chris started to shiver. "You've got a fever," Dad said quickly. "Where do you feel bad?"

"My head hurts, and I ache all over."

"Did you eat anything unusual yesterday?"

"No, not a thing. Just the school lunch and what we had for supper."

"Too much of anything?"

"No. I wasn't very hungry yesterday."

"Any pain in your stomach?"

"No. Now I'm getting cold." He pulled up the covers restlessly. "Dad," he said, through teeth beginning to chatter, "do something to make me well quick. I've got to go to school tomorrow."

Dad laughed a little. "Got to go to school tomorrow? That's a different story from the one I was hearing a few weeks ago. What is it, a test?"

"No, not a test. Jack and Freddie are choosing sides for the ball teams for Field Day."

"I'm afraid you won't be able to go tomorrow, Chris."

"I've just got to go, Dad! If I'm not there, nobody will choose me, and I'll be right back where I started. I'll be just a nothing again!"

"Have you been lying here worrying about that? Don't, Chris. I'll phone Miss Mayes, and she can explain to the boys and make sure you're chosen."

"No, Dad, that won't work," Chris stammered. By this time he was shaking so hard the whole bed rattled.

"Well, we're going to phone the doctor now. You've got a chill, that's plain, and I don't know what to do for you. So we'll get a doctor."

He took the blanket from his bed and spread it over Chris. Then he went out into the hall and telephoned.

78

It seemed forever before the doctor came. Chris stopped being cold and started burning up again. But all he could think about was missing his chance to be on Freddie's team.

"Doctor," he said, "can you fix me up so that I can go to school tomorrow?"

"Got a young scholar here?" the doctor asked Dad, sticking a thermometer in Chris's mouth.

"No," Dad answered, "a baseball player."

"Well, he'll have to postpone his baseball for three or four days. But that won't be bad, season's still young," the doctor replied, feeling and thumping Chris. Then he began asking questions.

When he had finished, he opened his black bag "It's a touch of the virus that's been going around," he said. "He'll probably run a fever for a couple of days. I'll give him a shot now, and in the morning I'll send him some medicine, a liquid to take every four hours and tablets every two hours. Keep him on a soft diet and see that he stays in bed a full day after he's free of fever."

Dad went out into the hall with the doctor. Chris began to shake with cold again. He was utterly miserable in body and soul. To have to miss a place on the team — it just wasn't fair!

Dad came back into the room. "Well, Chris, we have it all arranged," he said cheerfully."

"You mean I can go tomorrow?"

"Oh, no. Not tomorrow, but in a few days. Now go to sleep."

In the morning Dad brought Chris a bowl of hot cereal. "Doc says you're not sick enough to go to the hospital," he said, "and he doesn't know of any nurse we can get to come to the house, but he suggested a woman who has agreed to come, a baby sitter."

"A baby sitter? Oh, Dad!" Chris wailed.

"Well, I can't leave you here alone, and the work at the rig is at a stage where I've got to be there today. So this seems like a good solution."

"But, Dad, a baby sitter at my age! I'll never be able to live it down! The kids will never quit teasing me!"

"They won't even have to know unless you tell them. And she isn't coming to baby sit; she's coming to nurse you. Besides, she's the only one I know to get."

"I don't need anybody. I'll be all right staying by myself."

"I can't leave you to take the medicine by yourself. You might be groggy and take too much or not enough."

"Dad, you can't do this to me!"

"I'm not doing it to you. I'm doing it for you. Just be calm and sensible, Chris. Now I'll phone Margaret Mayes and ask her about the team."

80

"No, Dad, no! That will make it worse than ever! You don't understand!"

"I sure don't. I'm only trying to help you and take care of you. But if you don't want me to call, I won't."

A knock sounded on their door. "That must be Mrs. Lennon now."

"Mrs. Lennon! You mean Mrs. Lemon!"

"Chris, don't be a baby. The way you're acting you need a baby sitter. Now you be polite to Mrs. Lennon."

He went to the door and met her. He explained the situation and then brought her over to Chris.

"Mrs. Lennon," he said, "this is Chris. We both appreciate your helping us out."

"The poor boy! He does have a fever," Mrs. Lennon murmured. "Don't you worry, either of you. I'll have Chris comfortable in a jiffy, and he'll be well before you know it."

"I'm late now," said Dad, "so I'll leave him to you. See you this evening, Chris."

Mrs. Lennon was a friendly woman with a pleasant smile. "Now don't you worry," she repeated to Chris, "I've raised three boys of my own, so I know just how it is with boys. I'll get you comfy and give you your medicine, and then you can go off to sleep. That way the bad time will pass quicker."

While she talked, she fluffed his pillows and straightened the bed covers and took away the scarcely tasted bowl of cereal. Chris admitted to himself unwillingly that he did feel more comfortable. But his mind was still full of the humiliation of having a baby sitter and the disappointment of losing a chance to be on the team.

In spite of Mrs. Lennon's efforts, the day was a miserable one, filled with bad dreams when he dozed and worried thoughts when he was awake. But a little while after Dad came home and Mrs. Lennon left, his fever began to go down.

By next morning he felt all right, except for his worry about school. He was well enough to be bored and to wish he had something to read.

Mrs. Lennon came with a black and white kitten for him to play with. "I'm not giving him to you," she said, "just lending him for the day. I thought you might like to play with him. He's at the cute age."

"Oh, I do," Chris said, feeling the little cat under his hand vibrate from purring.

With the antics of the kitten and Mrs. Lennon's stories about her three boys, John in Germany, George in Japan, and Ernest in college, the time in bed passed more pleasantly than Chris had thought possible. Mrs. Lennon's good cooking helped too, for Chris was really hungry again. Dad always cooked things that took only a few minutes, but she cooked dishes that took a long time. He couldn't get enough of her chicken and dump-lings and stewed peaches and sweet potatoes with marshmallows.

She even baked him a batch of cookies. "These are light eating," she said, "wouldn't hurt a fly. Every boy ought to have a jar full of cookies all the time."

After school Miss Mayes came by with an armload of library books and a custard for him. "I made it myself," she said, "especially for you. I have something for you from the class too. Some of the boys wanted to bring it to you, but since you have a virus I was afraid their mothers wouldn't want them to come." She handed him a package that looked like a roll of notebook paper.

"Thank you," said Chris, and began to unroll it. It was a series of letters to him, pasted one after the other.

"Well, what do you know!" Chris exclaimed, grin-ning happily. "Look, Mrs. Lennon, a lot of letters from my class!"

Mrs. Lennon came to the door of the kitchen, a paring knife in her hand. "Well, isn't that nice," she said warmly.

"I'm going to start at the beginning and read straight through."

"Fine," said Mrs. Lennon. "Let me prop you up good and comfortable with pillows."

Miss Mayes said she had to leave. After she had

gone Chris settled himself among the pillows and began reading his letters with shy, unbelieving pleasure. "Can this really be me?" he wondered. "Did the class really do all this for me?"

He couldn't help looking for some unpleasant surprise; he didn't dare give himself over to complete enjoyment. But letter after letter was friendly and funny. When he passed Jack's, he breathed a little sigh of relief. It was short, but there was nothing in it to hurt his feelings. He began to let himself go then, snuggling deeper into the pillows and chuckling aloud at some of the jokes the kids wrote or the funny pictures they drew to illustrate their letters.

When he came to Freddie's letter, he read it twice, it was so wonderful. It said:

"Chris, you big lug, what do you mean by catching a germ when you ought to be out on the diamond catching flies? We chose sides yesterday, and of course you're on my team. I won the toss and got to choose first, and you were it. I got Pedro and Tom too, but Jack got Cotton. So hurry and come back to school so we can practice with all our first-string men.

Your friend,
"Freddie"

Chosen the very first one! And he'd been scared sick he wouldn't be chosen at all! That Freddie! What a great guy he was! What a wonderful friend!

He let the letters fall and just lay there thinking about the wonderfulness of it. I'm the luckiest guy in the world to have a friend like Freddie, he thought, the luckiest guy in the world!

After a while he picked up the letters again and read them to the end. In one way or another each one said, "We're sorry you are sick, and we hope you'll be back in school soon." Then he slowly rolled them together again, counting them. "Thirty-four," he said, coming to the last one and snapping the rubber band around the roll. "Every kid in the room wrote to me!"

He felt like a different person. He felt brave and lighthearted and strong. He jumped out of bed to get his mitt just to enjoy the feel of it, and was surprised to find his knees weak and trembly.

"But that doesn't count," he said, climbing back into bed. "I'm well again. I'll get strong again quick. I'll eat lots. By Monday I'll be strong again for sure. Mrs. Lemon, will you bring me Miss Mayes's custard, please?"

After he had eaten the custard, he took the rubber band off the letters and began rereading the best ones, enjoying them all over again, the jokes and riddles and news. When Dad came home, Chris was still reading. He was so flushed and bright-eyed that Dad thought he had a fever again and felt his forehead anxiously.

85

"Just look, Dad," said Chris, holding up the letters, "letters from my class! Just think, Dad, every single one in my class wrote to me! Isn't that something?"

"Yes, son," said Dad understandingly. "It's really something!"

"Oh, Dad, I like it here in Oakdale. I think it's the best school I was ever in. I hope we never have to leave here!"

8

Week End at Freddie's

The day Chris came back to school Freddie called him aside. "Say, Oily," he said, "how about you and me organizing a club?"

"Yes," said Chris at once. "Let's!"

"We could make it some kind of hunters' club and not let many in, just a few."

"Yes," Chris agreed again, "only a few of the best hunters."

"Not more than five, counting us. And we'll make the rules first, and they'll have to swear to keep them."

"Yes, and we'll have to think of a good name."

The bell rang, and they walked toward class. "You

be thinking," said Freddie, "but don't tell anybody. We'll plan some more tomorrow. We want this to be a ripsnorting club!"

Next morning Freddie passed a note to Chris. "Come and spend this week end with me," it said. "Then we can plan our club. Mom said I could invite you."

"Thanks, I'd like to," Chris wrote back. "But I'll have to ask my dad."

Dad was a little embarrassing about it. He insisted on phoning Freddie's mother, but after talking to her, he gave Chris permission to go.

Chris rode out on the school bus with Freddie, his clean clothes instead of books bulging his briefcase.

They got off the bus at their gate with Freddie's three little sisters trailing after them. "Let's hurry," said Freddie. "We don't have to wait for the girls. If we hurry, we'll have time to look at my traps before milking time."

They ran down the lane to the house, a comfortable-looking two-storied white frame building about half a mile from the gate.

"Hey, Mom, I'm home," Freddie called, flinging his books on the front porch. "Chris is with me."

"In here," Mrs. Felsing called back. They went into the living room, where Mrs. Felsing was mending while she listened to the radio. Freddie's baby brother, Jimmy, played on the floor with a train.

Mrs. Felsing was a friendly looking woman, with curly hair and blue eyes like Freddie's.

"Any cookies, Mom?" Freddie asked.

"On the kitchen table," she said, and the boys were soon off to check the traps, carrying cookies in both hands.

The first trap was untouched. There was a cottontail in the next one. The third trap was sprung but empty. There was a possum in the fourth trap and another rabbit in the last one.

They set the traps again and hurried home with their catch, for Freddie had to do his regular evening chores. Chris helped him put out feed for the cattle and then sat and watched him as he milked three cows.

It was dark by the time they finished and went into the kitchen.

Freddie put the bucket of milk on the table, got his hand slapped playfully as he grabbed a cookie, and, laughing, started a friendly scuffle with Chris.

"Hey, there," said Mrs. Felsing, "none of that in my kitchen, Sonny. I don't want those big shovels you call your feet flying around and knocking my cups off the shelf."

Freddie stopped scuffling and began walking the kitchen stiffly as a robot. "My steam shovels," he explained to Chris with mock dignity. He lifted his feet in slow, rhythmical precision. You could almost see them scoop up a load of dirt.

At supper that night Chris decided that the Felsings were the jolliest family he had ever seen. Everybody laughed and joked. Freddie teased the girls, and they all teased him — not mean, hurtful teasing, but the funny kind. Mr. Felsing joked with all of them, and everybody laughed at the baby as if he were the most wonderful little clown in the world.

After supper Freddie and Chris went out into the barn and skinned the animals they had caught. Then they scraped the hides and fastened them to the wall to dry until they were ready for the next step in tanning.

Afterwards they went upstairs to Freddie's room and read funny books till bedtime.

Next morning Freddie was up at dawn to do his chores of feeding and milking, Chris with him.

At breakfast Mr. Felsing said, "Freddie, you and Chris can ride fence in the creek pasture today."

"But, Daddy," Freddie objected, "I thought Chris and I would go hunting this morning."

"I'm sorry, but I need your help. But when you finish that pasture, the rest of the day is yours."

"May we take our guns?"

"No. I want you to be looking for loose wires and break-throughs in the fence. You can't do a good job if you're looking for rabbits and varmints too. Chris, can you ride?"

"A little. But I haven't been on a horse for over a year."

"You'd better saddle Fritz for Chris, then, Freddie."

"Okay," he agreed, "but that will be about as exciting as cold potatoes."

It was much more exciting to Chris. Riding horseback through the pasture was fun. Freddie rode unconcerned among the cattle, but Chris couldn't help feeling a little thrill of danger. He liked, too, the feeling of importance he had when he helped Freddie use the wire stretcher to tighten a loose wire and patch up a break so the cattle wouldn't get out before Mr. Felsing could string new wire. It was fun to be doing real, useful man's work.

They finished by ten-thirty, then ran and reset the traps. They had caught only two skunks, and Freddie didn't want to save the skins.

"I know what let's do," said Freddie. "Let's shoot crows."

"Why crows?"

"Because the county pays a bounty on crows. Hey, that's poetry! The county pays a bounty!" He began singing it like a grand opera soprano, striking a pose of grandeur.

91

"The county pays a bounty
Because crows are its foes.
They eat corn 'fore it grows.
So the county pays a bounty!"
His voice cracked on a high note.

"You fool," Chris said, laughing. "How much do they pay?"

"Forty cents a pair of feet," Freddie continued singing.

"And I say that is very neat!
In fact, it's really hard to beat.
The money'll give us quite a treat,
Because the county pays a bounty!"

"Aw, come on," said Chris. "Let's get started!"

They got their guns and took up positions at the edge of the garden. It was only a few minutes until they shot their first crow. The rest flew away and didn't come back. So they went over to the corn field and shot there, then went back to the garden.

Once they heard a noisy cackling from the chicken yard. "I'll bet that's the hawk that's been getting Mom's baby chicks," said Freddie. "Come on, let's hurry!"

They raced to the chicken yard. All the hens were cackling and clucking in great excitement. Some were sitting with widespread wings covering their brood. Half grown broilers were running long-legged for the shelter of weeds or chicken houses. A big hawk was just rising from the far corner.

"Look, he's got one," Freddie cried. "Shoot!"

Chris could see the chick struggling in the talons of the hawk. Both boys shot at almost the same instant, and the hawk fell to the ground.

The chick escaped unhurt and began a fearful cheeping. Freddie went over and shooed it back to the chicken yard. The chickens seemed to know that the danger was over. Baby chicks ran out from under the hens, and the hens rose and began scratching for food as if nothing had happened.

"Well, that's our good deed for today," said Freddie. "Mom will sure be glad that hawk is out of the way forever!"

After that they went back and forth between the garden and the corn field until the dinner bell rang. By that time Chris had shot five crows, Freddie six.

Mrs. Felsing served a wonderful dinner of chicken and dumplings, cole slaw and carrots crisp and fresh from the garden, and deep-dish apple pie with cream. Then the family began to get ready to go to town.

"But, Daddy, we don't want to go to town. We're in town every day of the week. There's nothing to do in town. It's no fun on a day like this!"

"Okay, Robinson Crusoe," said Mr. Felsing. "Stay

here in the wide open spaces, then. But remember, while we're gone there'll be no shooting, no swimming, no riding. Is that understood?"

"But, Daddy, we can take care of ourselves!"

"Is that understood?" Mr. Felsing repeated.

"Yes, sir," Freddie said.

And so after Chris had beaten Freddie three out of five at checkers and they had made lemonade and eaten cookies, they stretched out on the grass under the pecan trees just talking, once in a while wrestling a little.

"Forty cents a pair for crow's feet isn't bad," said Freddie, chewing on a blade of grass. "I just wish there wasn't a limit of ten pairs to a person."

"But anyway we can each make four dollars."

"I wonder what else the government pays a bounty on."

"Down in South Texas they pay for wolves. And just the other day I read that in Baltimore they pay twenty-five cents a hundred for lightning bugs, and no limit to how many by one person," said Chris.

"Just imagine! I bet I could catch a thousand down at the tank any night."

"Easy!"

"I bet a man could make a living just going around hunting the varmints the government pays to have killed. Wouldn't be any work at all, hardly. Just fun."

94

"But it takes a long time for bounties on what we can hunt to amount to much," said Chris.

"I don't know. We've made four dollars and forty cents today, and that ain't hay."

"I know, but I still wish we could go out for something bigger."

"Yes, but what?"

They lay in silence, chewing on tender blades of grass. Chris forgot even to think as he listened to the lazy clank of the windmill turning slowly in the little breeze and watched the butterflies hovering over the tall white daisies in the long flower bed bordering the fence.

"I know one thing maybe we could get," said Freddie suddenly, sitting up.

"What?"

"A few days ago Daddy said he'd give fifty dollars to find out who's stealing our turkeys."

"Did he mean it?"

"Sounded like he did. He was good and mad."

"Why don't we find out who's doing it? Has somebody really been stealing your turkeys?"

"Sure looks like it. They're disappearing, anyway, one or two a day."

"Could some animal be getting them?"

"Daddy doesn't think so, because whatever it is doesn't get them at night but in the daytime."

"How do you know? Do you count them every day?"

"No, silly. There's over three hundred of them. Have you ever tried counting even fifty turkeys?"

"No," said Chris, picturing how hard it would be to count turkeys as they milled around in the flock. "But then how do you know the thief doesn't get them at night?"

"Because the turkeys roost in the live oaks down in the cow lot. Haven't you noticed? If anything tried to get them, they'd make a terrible commotion. We couldn't help hearing the squawking and the gobbling."

"I see. Where do they go in the daytime?"

"They graze all over the place. But mostly they wander south, down to the creek pasture and the live oak motte."

"Do they get out of the sight of the house?"

"Sure they do. Have you noticed them in the daytime? Did you see any of them when we were riding the fences this morning?"

"No, but I'm just asking," said Chris, a little hurt at Freddie's impatience. "I don't know anything about turkeys except that they're good to eat. I'm just trying to get the picture."

"Okay. What else do you want to know?"

"Couldn't someone follow them and catch the

96

thief? Sort of ride herd on them?"

"Who has time? Mom and Dad don't, and I'm in school."

"Except Saturday and Sunday. We could spy on them then."

"It would be a pretty dumb thief that wouldn't figure that out."

"What makes you think it's a person, not an animal?"

"Because animals generally get their prey in the dark."

"Does your Dad suspect anyone?"

"He hasn't said, but I think he does. I know I do."

"Who?"

"The man that lives south of us on the other side of the creek."

"Why do you think he's guilty?"

"Well, for one thing, the turkeys generally go over that way to feed, and there's lots of trees and brush so a person could sneak up on them and not be noticed. And for another thing, he has houses for his turkeys and a pen. Most of the farmers around here don't have houses for their turkeys. They just let them roost in the trees. He's not a very good farmer, either, about most things. But he has turkey houses and a pen fenced with chicken wire."

"I get it. You mean he could catch turkeys one or

two at a time and keep them in his pen till they got used to being with the new flock."

"Uh huh."

"Could you tell by looking at his flock?"

"No. He has the same breed we do, and turkeys all look alike to me."

"To me too. How does anyone ever tell?"

"Sometimes the farmer will put a dab of paint on each turkey, any bright color, sort of like a brand."

"But your dad doesn't?"

"No. Neither do the Frends. They're the ones I'm talking about."

"Seems sort of hopeless to prove anything, doesn't it?" Chris said.

"There is one thing I'd like to try. I've been thinking of it ever since Daddy began noticing that some of the turkeys were disappearing."

"What's that?"

"I'd like to put a dab of paint on every one of our turkeys under a wing so nobody would see it and then after a few days do a little quiet checking in the Frends' turkey pen."

"Say, that sounds like a good idea! Let's try it!" exclaimed Chris, sitting up.

"If Daddy really will pay the fifty dollar reward. Let's find out about that first."

"Let's do it anyway. It will be fun — exciting!"

"It'll be a lot of work, too, and I'd rather get paid for my work. Have you ever tried to catch a turkey, Chris?"

"No, but let's do it. Let's plan, anyway. This could be what our club could be for."

"Okay, let's plan. And let's do make it a club. Only let's not just make it a club to get a reward for catching a turkey thief. Instead of a hunting club, let's make it a club for collecting rewards and bounties on anything."

"Okay, let's. And we'll think up a name and secret password and everything. Who will we ask to join?"

"Let's have just a few, mostly those that like to hunt. Hey, I've just thought of something. The more boys in the club, the more ways we'll have to split our reward and bounty money. Let's make it a very exclusive club and have its only members you and me!"

"Suits me fine," agreed Chris, his eyes shining. "What shall we call it?"

"Let's have three words with initials that spell something, like BUD or PAL or ACE."

"B for bounty."

"P for partners."

"C for chums."

"One for each word. But I can't think of any other words to go with them. Can you?"

Chris thought hard. "No, I can't," he admitted finally. "Not right now."

"Never mind. We'll think of something. Now let's plan how we can get started with the turkeys. The easiest time to catch them is at night when they're roosting."

"Let's do it tonight."

"Let's start tonight," said Freddie. "It'll take us more than one night to finish the whole flock."

"Just a dab on each?"

"Sure, just a dab. But one of us will have to hold the turkey and raise its wing while the other one puts on the paint."

"Do you have any paint?"

"Oh, yes, there's always some left-over paint in the tool shed. Brushes, too."

"Let's get it ready."

"All right, let's," agreed Freddie, getting up and stretching.

9

The Pals

That night at the supper table Freddie brought up the question of the reward. "Daddy," he asked, "did you really mean it the other day when you said you'd give fifty dollars to find out what was happening to your turkeys?"

"Sure I meant it. I've lost more than that already, counting the market price of the grown bird. And if it goes on, I'll probably lose twice as much. Sure I meant it. But don't get me started on the turkeys. I'm feeling good, and I want to enjoy my supper."

"Okay," said Freddie quickly. "But Chris and I thought we'd put a dab of left-over red paint on each turkey. Is that all right with you?"

"Yes, yes. Can't do any harm, might help. Mom, did you see Mrs. Reuter in town this afternoon? She was looking for you."

While Freddie's parents talked about Mrs. Reuter, Chris and Freddie tried out words for their club name.

"Active," said Freddie.

"Loyal," said Chris.

"Lads."

"Detectives."

"I like the one starting with 'partner,' " said Chris. "Let's work on it."

"What are you talking about?" asked Betty.

"Private business," said Freddie.

"Mom," said Betty, "Freddie and Chris are saying words to each other. Not sentences, just words! Make them tell me what they mean!"

"Oh, Mom, it's secret," Freddie objected.

"Well, if it's secret, don't tantalize Betty at the supper table. Wait till you're alone."

As soon as supper was over, Chris and Freddie started for the turkey roosts, stopping at the tool shed for a can of red paint, a small paint brush, and a flashlight.

"I've thought of something that fits," said Chris as they walked along. "Partners Are Loyal. PAL."

"Hey, that's pretty good," said Freddie. "Or Partners Are Lucky. That's what we hope. But I bet we'll think of something even better."

When they reached the cow lot, they saw that most of the turkeys had settled on low branches or the tops of the fences and could be easily reached. But catching them was only the beginning. Chris soon learned that marking a turkey did indeed run into work, as Freddie had prophesied.

Freddie, being more experienced, would grab the turkeys. Most of them were young birds from this spring's hatching, but even these half-grown birds kicked and clawed and flapped their wings and pecked. And they kept up a continual gobble-gobble, in which all the other turkeys in the flock joined them.

Freddie would struggle with the turkey until he held it firmly with its right wing raised. Chris, holding the flashlight in his left hand, would dab a generous blob of red paint under the wing. Then the bird would be released to fly back to its roost, protesting at the top of its voice.

Freddie tried to go down the row on each branch, but when he grabbed one turkey and pulled it down, half a dozen others would fly down too. When they flew back up, it was more than likely to a place on the limb that Freddie had already passed. It was difficult to know which turkeys had been marked and which hadn't, and the boys found themselves handling the same bird several times.

They couldn't talk to each other without shouting, so they began concentrating all their efforts on their task and soon had a sort of assembly line going. Freddie would grab the turkey, tuck its head under his left arm, hold it with his left hand, raise its wing with his right, and Chris would be ready on the instant with his dab of paint.

They worked doggedly for forty-five minutes, the gobbling and flapping of wings ringing in their ears, and then decided to exchange jobs. But it didn't work as smoothly with Chris holding the birds. He didn't have Freddie's knack of catching the turkey and holding it in just the right position. Invariably a wing would slap his face, a claw scratch him, or an angry bill peck him. He lost so much time that Freddie soon suggested that they change jobs again.

"I told you it would run into work," Freddie yelled. "This is worth fifty dollars!"

"Sure is," Chris yelled back, rubbing his cheek where a turkey had just pecked him.

But they kept on. At first they had tried to count the birds they marked, but they soon lost count and gave that up. The turkeys began flying to higher branches, and the boys had to get them down by throwing small pieces of wood at them. When they were knocked off balance, the turkeys would flop down with an outraged squawk and much flapping of wings.

Finally, when Chris's arm was beginning to tremble from holding the flashlight for so long, Freddie shouted, "We've done about half of them. Let's leave the rest for tomorrow night."

"Okay, let's," Chris shouted back quickly.

When they went into the living room, Mr. Felsing had a suggestion. "Why don't you get up early in the morning," he asked, "before the turkeys start to wander off, and let them out of the gate one at a time?"

Freddie struck his forehead in disgust for himself. "Why didn't I think of that?" he asked. "It's so simple! That will work much better. We won't be catching the same turkey over and over, and we can be sure we're not missing any. Come on, Chris. Let's go back and close the gate now so they won't beat us out in the morning."

Up in Freddie's room at last, they set the alarm and crawled into bed. For a long time before he fell asleep the sound of gobbling and squawking rang again in Chris's ears, the strong musky odor of the turkeys lingered in his memory, and his skin itched with the feeling that turkey mites were crawling on him.

The next morning the boys were back at their turkey

105

marking by dawn. The work went easier and smoother as they let the turkeys out of the gate one by one. There was still a bedlam of gobbling, but this morning it was not so nerve-wracking, being the mutterings of complaint rather than the screams of fear. But it was almost church time before they finished.

"We're sure going to a lot of work to get that loot," Freddie said as they walked toward the house.

"Loot!" exclaimed Chris. "L! Partners After Loot! PAL!"

"Partners After Loot!" Freddie repeated. "That gets it, the reward and bounties and all. That's good!" He stuck out his hand. "Hi, PAL!" he said.

"Hi, PAL!" Chris echoed, shaking hands solemnly. "They'll never guess what the letters stand for!"

They lost no time letting the boys at school know about the club. They printed PAL on their book covers and notebooks. They wore their sleeves rolled up to show ink tattoos of PAL on their arms, being careful to put the ink on at home, because if Miss Mayes saw anyone putting on ink tattoos in school, she made him wash it off.

Of course all VI-3 was very curious and begged to know what PAL stood for, but Chris and Freddie kept the secret and had everyone guessing. Somebody guessed "partners" but nobody guessed "loot," and their secret was safe. Tom and Cotton and Pedro and half a dozen other boys, even Jack, wanted to join the club. But Chris and Freddie were firm and refused to admit anyone else. It was lots of fun.

They wished they didn't have to wait until Saturday to check up on the Frends and collect their reward. But they were so busy practicing baseball for Field Day that they didn't even have time to sit down and plan how they would go about it. They left all that for Friday night.

Chris made sure early in the week that he could spend the weekend with Freddie again.

"We can't let this become a habit. We can't impose on the Felsings," Dad said when Chris asked him, and Chris's heart sank. "But," Dad went on, "it will suit me fine for you to have some place to stay this week end because I have to go to San Antonio on business and won't be back till Monday."

Thursday night Dad came in quietly and undressed without turning on the light. But once in bed he twisted and tossed so restlessly that the bedsprings creaked noisily enough to wake Chris.

He lay for a few minutes trying to decide what had roused him. Then he whispered, "Dad, are you feeling sick?"

"No, Chris. I'm not sick."

"Then what's the matter?"

"I'm worried, Chris. I might as well tell you and get it over with. Turn on the light."

"Why don't we just talk in the dark? It's sort of cozy."

"No. For this we'd better see each other's faces."

Chris switched on the light. Dad lay facing him, propped on his elbow.

"What's the matter, Dad?"

"It's that we're coming to two big changes in our life, Chris," Dad said slowly, feeling his way for words. "One change is for sure. I've decided on it But the other change I can't make up my mind about."

"What's the change for sure?"

"That I'm going to marry Margaret Mayes. I reckon you have guessed that, the way I've been seeing her lately."

Chris felt as if someone had hit him in the stomach. "No, Dad. I guess I've been too busy with Freddie to notice. I thought she was just like the other girls you went out with."

"Well, she's not. You're glad about it, aren't you, Son?"

"I don't know," Chris said slowly. "It's going to be awfully funny to have a teacher around the house."

"It's going to be nice. Besides, she won't be a teacher after we're married. She'll be my wife and your mother."

"Will I have to call her mother?"

"No. She's not old enough to be your real mother. We thought you'd just like to call her Margaret."

Chris felt as if everything was topsy-turvy, as if he were in a boat rocking in the storm.

"Will she boss me around?"

"No, Chris. You'll have to remember all this change will be as new and strange to her as it is to you. She won't want to boss you. She'll want to be your friend. She'll want to be like a big sister. Chris, you like her, don't you?"

"Yes, but I never thought about her as your wife."

"She likes you, Chris. The three of us will get along fine. We'll be happier than we've ever been."

"I'm happy now. We have good times together. We get along fine. Why do we have to have anyone else?"

"Chris, I told you to start with that this was one change that I have decided. I hope you'll like it. I know you will when you get used to the idea. Margaret said she wouldn't marry me unless you gave your consent. I told her nuts to that. A man's kid doesn't pick his wife. Whether you want me to or not, I'm going to marry Margaret Mayes. That's settled."

Chris began to feel safe again. If Dad said a thing was settled, it was settled. He might as well make the best of it. It might be fun. What would Freddie think? Wouldn't Freddie be surprised to know Miss Mayes was going to be his stepmother?

Thinking of it, Chris smiled. "Okay, Dad," he said. "That's settled. What's the other part?"

Dad smiled too and lay back. "The other part is where we're going to live."

"You mean maybe we can live in a real house instead of just an apartment?"

"Yes, but I mean more than that." He pounded his pillow into a ball. "Chris, you're happy here in Oakdale, aren't you? Happier than you've ever been?"

"Dad," Chris cried, sitting up in bed, "you mean we have to leave Oakdale? Is the well dry? Can't you get any more locations here?"

"It's dry, and we can't get any more locations. But we may not have to leave Oakdale."

"Good," Chris said, lying down again. "I was scared for a minute. I thought you meant I'd have to leave Freddie and all the kids at school and our club and baseball and everything."

Dad was quiet, just looking at him. It made Chris start to think. "But, Dad," he said, "if there are no more wells to drill, what will you do here?"

"I have a chance to get a job here buying leases. Chris, the trouble is I have a chance to get two jobs, one here that won't be quite as good as the one I have, and the other one a promotion that would still keep me moving from place to place. Chris, I want you to be happy. I don't know if I have the right to tear you away from Oakdale when it's become home to you. I can't decide this by myself. You have to help me."

"I want to stay, Dad."

"We have to be sure what's best in the long run."

"What does Miss Mayes say?"

"She says it's for you and me to decide; she'll be happy with us wherever we live."

"Then that's settled too. We'll stay!"

"Yes," said Dad slowly, "it seems that that's settled too."

10

The Problem

Next morning at school Chris watched for a chance
to see Miss Mayes alone. It came sooner than he expected, just after the first bell rang. She walked over to
the drinking fountain, and no one else was there. Chris
followed her quickly.

"Hi, Margaret," he whispered as she stooped to
drink.

She straightened quickly and looked at him. "You
know?" she asked, "Greg told you? You're glad!" She
put her hands on his shoulders. "Oh, Chris," she said,
"I'm so glad that you're glad!"

And Chris found that he was glad. It was exciting

112

to think that a girl as beautiful as Margaret Mayes was coming to live with them. And she's as good as she is beautiful, he thought, in the old fairy tale words.

It was exciting, too, to know that they would live in Oakdale and he wouldn't have to leave Freddie and the gang.

It was a good, comfortable feeling to have everything settled.

And everything would have been settled if he and Dad had talked in the dark. But Chris had seen Dad's face, and that morning in reading class he remembered the look on it. It wouldn't let him feel completely happy about staying in Oakdale. It even kept him from telling Freddie the good news.

He forgot about it during recess and language arts, but in arithmetic period there was Dad's face again, with the unhappy eyes. It made Chris start to think.

What would the Oakdale job mean to Dad?

Why didn't he want to stay in Oakdale? Surely he would be happier too, settled in a house with things around to stay the way they wanted them. Surely he would enjoy having friends he could go fishing with and play golf with and invite over for back-yard barbecues, especially with Margaret to keep house for him.

Why wasn't he happy about it?

"The one here won't be quite as good as the job I

have," Dad had said. Chris thought what the Oakdale job would be. Buying leases. Suddenly he remembered what he had heard Dad say many a time, without paying any attention to it.

"When I get too old to be a driller any more, I'll get a job buying leases." That's what Dad had said, again and again. But Dad wasn't old. It wasn't time for him to quit being a driller!

Then there was the money, too. Dad had said he wouldn't be making quite as much money if he stayed in Oakdale. That was all right with Chris. They'd have enough. He'd rather stay where people liked him, where he knew the kids and they knew him, where he *belonged,* then to have a new car every other year and expensive model kits and guns and things.

But how did Dad feel about it? With a sinking heart Chris put himself in Dad's place. He would feel that he was not doing his best, especially when he turned down a promotion. He would feel like a failure.

Chris didn't think this out all at once, and his mind wasn't constantly thinking about Dad. But when he wasn't busy — and sometimes even when he was — he saw the look in Dad's eyes.

Chris didn't want to admit it, but he had to. Dad was willing to be unhappy himself to make his son happy. It made Chris feel proud and sad at the same time.

It was Friday evening, and he was spending the weekend with Freddie when he reached this conclusion.

He was sitting waiting, watching while Freddie milked. The evening coolness and the rich, clean scent of the barn and the rhythmic sound of the milk squirting into the bucket made it a good time for thinking. He got this far in his problem and then Freddie asked him a question and he forgot all about Dad and leaving Oakdale. Right after supper he and Freddie were going to plan how to go to the Frends'.

As soon as they had finished their second pieces of peach pie, the boys went up to Freddie's room and settled down for a long discussion. "One thing's for sure," Freddie started. "We can't go to the Frends' before sundown because the turkeys don't come home to roost before then."

"How do we know the Frends won't be there?"

"Because they always go to town right after dinner Saturday afternoon and stay until after the movie that night. They'll be getting home about ten o'clock."

"It gets dark a little before eight," said Chris. "So that gives us about two hours. But what if they don't go to town this Saturday?"

"Then we'll just have to wait until next Saturday."

"How can we tell?"

"We'll have to watch for their car going to town

about one o'clock. We can see it go down the highway from our front porch. It's a green Ford."

"Okay. So we know they're not at home. How do we get away from here?"

"I've thought about that a lot," Freddie admitted. "That's one of the hardest parts."

"Can't we just tell your dad what we want to do?"

"No. We're not going to do anything wrong, but I just feel it in my bones he wouldn't let us go if he knew."

"I bet you'll feel it in your bones when he does find out! Wham!"

"I'll just have to take that chance. I've been on trips to the woodshed before."

"If he wallops you, you can have an extra five dollars."

"Okay, it's a deal."

"My dad hasn't walloped me since I was ten years old."

"What had you done then?"

"Copied on a test at school. Never again! But if we can't let them know we're going, how can we get away from the house?"

"I think the best thing we can do is just say we are going for a ride in the moonlight. It will be full moon tomorrow, and Daddy knows you like to ride old Fritz. We just won't say anything about where we're going."

"That sounds all right to me. I've sort of not been liking the idea of walking through the weedy pastures and wading the creek at night."

"Riding will be better. We can get away from the Frends quicker if they should come home unexpectedly, too."

"Okay. That gets us there and takes us away. What are we going to do while we're there?"

"Catch every turkey and lift its right wing to find the dab of red paint. If we find even one or two, we can stop, because that will prove that the Frends have been stealing our turkeys."

"We'll have to take flashlights."

"Yes. I have two, mine and Daddy's. The Frends have three turkey houses. You'll take one and I'll take one, and if we haven't found any painted turkeys by the time we've finished those two, we'll both work in the third house."

"Couldn't we catch the turkeys one at a time as they come into the pen, the way we let them out last week? Wouldn't that be easier than grabbing them off the roost?"

"Yes, but we'd have to start before dark to do that. I don't want anyone to see us."

"Well, then, that's all set," said Chris, thinking with distaste of the stale odor and flopping wings in store for him. "All we have to do to get ready to go is to get the flashlights and saddle the horses."

"One other thing," said Freddie. "The Frends have a dog."

"Oh, oh! What do we do about that?"

"Well, Bozo knows me. I don't think he'll give us any trouble. But just to be sure, I'm going to take him a hunk of meat from the deepfreeze."

Chris lay awake a long time before he went to sleep that night. His thoughts were a troubled jumble of worries about his and Freddie's Saturday night venture and his and Dad's problem.

Both boys were glad that Mr. Felsing had work for them to do all Saturday morning; it made the time pass quicker. After dinner they sat on the front porch and watched the highway until they saw the Frends' green Ford pass on the way to town. So far, so good!

But Saturday afternoon dragged. They could not get interested in anything. Nothing was fun because they kept thinking about that night at the Frends'. All they could think of to do was to eat. They emptied the cookie jar and began on the refrigerator, and the more they ate, the lazier they felt.

A little before five o'clock the phone rang. "Freddie," asked Mrs. Felsing, "would you and Chris mind staying alone this evening until about nine-thirty?"

"No," Freddie answered. "We wouldn't mind at all."

"It's the first time we've left you alone at night, but with Chris here, the two of you ought to be all right. You see, it turns out Cousin Anna is in town just till tomorrow morning, and the Ahmbrents want us to have supper with them."

"Sure, Mom. You all go right ahead. Chris and I will be fine."

"Are you sure you won't be afraid?" Mom asked.

"What do you think we are, a couple of sissies?"

"Well, I guess it will be all right. And we do want to visit with Cousin Anna. You be careful. Daddy says be sure to tend to all the work. And if you need anything, phone us at Ahmbrents'. The number is 697. Write it down."

"Sure, Mom. Don't you worry about a thing."

Freddie hung up the receiver with a shout. "Hey, Chris, old boy," he said, "we're all set! The road is cleared before us! Everything's ripsnorting!"

The boys ate again. Then they tended to the evening chores early. It was still not seven o'clock when they finished, but they saddled Fritz and Lightning and decided to ride until dark.

When they were a mile away from the house, they remembered the meat for Bozo and had to ride back for it. It was dusk when they finally rode up to the Frends'

119

turkey pen, first making sure there was no car in the garage.

Bozo raced barking to meet them. But when Freddie called his name and talked to him, he began wagging his tail as he barked. And when they threw him the chunk of meat, he let them get off their horses and go into the turkey yard without bothering them.

The turkeys had about settled down for the night. There were only a few sounds and an occasional fluttering to the ground as a greedy turkey shoved a weaker one off the perch. But a few minutes after the boys went to work, both houses were in an uproar. Turkeys that had not been touched gobbled and screamed as loud as those that had, and flew clumsily from one side of the house to another.

The boys soon found that they could not hold a turkey and look under its wing singlehanded. They had to work as a team again. Once more Freddie caught and held the turkeys while Chris, with his flashlight, looked for the red mark. Once more there was a bedlam of noise and flopping wings and turkey smell; only now, in the turkey house instead of the outdoors, the stench was nauseating.

They thought they would never get to the end of the row. They knew that several times they examined the same birds, but the stupid creatures wouldn't stay in line.

120

But they found not a single dab of red paint.

After a long time they finished the first house and came out. They took great gulps of the cool fresh air to clear their lungs of the stench.

"Not a single dab of red paint," said Chris doubtfully.

"Maybe the stolen ones are all together in the next house," said Freddie.

"I sure hate to go in to find out."

"Well, now we've gone this far, it would be silly not to go all the way," Freddie said. "Come on. Time's a-wasting!"

They plunged into the second house. Noise and flapping and smell!

They finished with faces and arms scratched and Chris's shirt torn, but no red-marked turkeys.

"We might as well quit," Chris said. But Freddie was determined to go on.

But when they were half way through the last house without finding a red dab, Freddie shouted, "None of these turkeys has a mark. We've made a mistake."

"Yes," Chris shouted back. "Besides, it must be getting late. We don't want to get caught here."

"But let's keep on to the bitter end to be sure," Freddie decided.

They did, but they found no red-marked turkeys.

They came out of the house running, closed the gate to the pen, and jumped on their horses. They gulped the fresh air greedily. Suddenly they were in a panic for fear the Frends might come and find them.

They rode away fast, loping their horses at first. Bozo ran along beside them, barking, giving them a great send-off. But as soon as they knew they were safely away, they slowed down to a walk.

"Well, I was sure wrong about the Frends," said Freddie. "There goes fifty dollars' worth of work!"

"What do we do next?"

"I don't know. I was so sure we'd find stolen turkeys at the Frends' that I didn't plan any farther."

"I guess we'll just have to hide and watch the turkeys in the daytime," Chris suggested.

"I guess so. We can start tomorrow. Look, that car's turning in at our gate! Hurry!"

But Freddie's folks reached the house before the boys did. Mr. Felsing was waiting for them as they rode up.

"Where have you been, young man?" he asked angrily. "Your mother gets worried about leaving you here alone and phones, and no answer. So of course we have to get up and leave at once. Where have you been?"

Freddie told him. "But you don't have to worry about the Frends any more," he ended. "They're not getting your turkeys."

"I don't have to worry!" Mr. Felsing shouted. "I don't have to worry! My son sneaks into my neighbor's turkey pen at night, and I don't have to worry!"

"But I was only trying to help you. Now that we've proved he didn't steal the turkeys, he won't ever have to know we suspected him."

"The only reason I don't march you straight over there to apologize is because I'm too ashamed for him to know."

"But, Daddy, I thought you suspected him too."

"I did, but I certainly wasn't going to have a falling out with my neighbor over a few turkeys. I'd rather lose five hundred dollars worth of turkeys than make enemies of the Frends. And that's what would have happened if he'd caught you."

"But he didn't. And I thought you'd feel better to know he isn't stealing your turkeys."

"I do," Mr. Felsing admitted, his face red with anger. "But it still makes me mad that you don't have any better judgment than to go over there the way you did. And two other things besides. You know you're not supposed to ride the horses when you're alone on the place. And the very first time we think you're old enough to be trusted to stay by yourself at night you pull a stunt like this. You've got several lessons to learn, young man, and I'm the fellow to teach you. Come with me."

He turned to Chris. "And for two cents," he said to him, "I'd teach you the same lessons!"

Chris kept quiet. But as he heard the belt falling, he thought he would have felt better if Mr. Felsing had walloped him too.

Freddie took it all philosophically. "What I got I guess I had coming to me," he said. "Any way you look at it, it isn't easy to earn fifty dollars."

"But we're right back where we started," Chris said, discouraged.

"No, we're not. We're ahead, because we've eliminated the Frends. I think we've eliminated all the rest of the people too, because I don't believe any of our other neighbors would go miles out of their way to steal one or two turkeys at a time. It just doesn't make sense."

"Then you think an animal must be getting them?"

"Must be. Anyway, we'll just have to watch like you said till we find out. I want that reward for PAL's!"

11

The Answer

Next day right after church they changed into their blue jeans and started on their new hunt. They didn't even wait to eat dinner. Mrs. Felsing let them take the first pieces of fried chicken that came from the pan, Freddie made bread and butter sandwiches, and each boy cut a big hunk of chocolate cake. They put the food in a paper sack and water in a thermos bottle and set out, stopping on their way through the garden to pick two ripe red tomatoes to add to their lunch. Besides their food, Freddie carried his BB gun and Chris his Benjamin pump.

It was very hot this midday under the broiling May

sun, and the boys squinted in the bright glare in spite of the big straw hats that shaded their faces. In their search for the turkeys they walked first through a small pasture overgrown with wild flowers. Along the fence that bordered the corn field orange camphor daisies and lavender American star thistles bloomed waist high, and red and yellow firewheels brushed against their knees. They were careful not to touch the dazzling white bull nettles and prickly poppies that grew in patches.

The boys did not talk much as they walked along. Perspiration was soon streaming down their faces, but Chris felt a sort of drowsy enjoyment in being out in the hot sunshine. The sun-baked pasture smelled good and clean and faintly sweet from the flowers, and a different kind of sweetness came from the corn field. Every once in a while a mockingbird trilled from a mesquite tree, and several times quail flew up ahead of them with a whir.

At last they crawled through the barbed wire fence at the end of the pasture and entered another pasture. Cattle were grazing, and there were no wild flowers, only grass and clumps of cactus and tall weeds and a few scattered scrubby mesquite trees.

Chris saw the turkeys first. They were in a busy, quiet bunch off to the left, bending their long necks to peer and peck choosily, then stalking on to peck again.

"Turkeys sure are stupid," Freddie said. "You'd

126

think on a hot day like this they'd find some shade to feed in. But no, they're out in the broiling sun, and that puts us there too."

"Let's walk over closer to them and get under one of the mesquites. That'll give us some shade."

"Mighty little," said Freddie, "but better than nothing. We've got to get out of this sun. It's baking every brain in my head."

They walked on. It was easier going here than in the flowery pasture, but Chris felt a little nervous as they approached half a dozen cattle grazing between them and the turkeys. Freddie was unconcerned, however, and Chris pretended to be too. The cows merely looked up as they passed, then went back to their grazing.

"This will be a good place for us to watch from," Freddie finally decided, stopping at a mesquite clump. "We'll be sort of hidden here, and we oughtn't to get any closer to the turkeys, or it will be too easy for the thief to spot us."

It was a very small mesquite clump but no smaller than most of those in the pasture, a big bush rather than a tree, and now, with the sun straight overhead, it cast only a small circle of shade. The boys had to crawl close to the trunk to get out of the sun. They settled down facing the turkeys with mesquite leaves tickling the backs of their necks.

"I can't stand that," said Freddie. He took out his pocket knife and hacked away at the small branches until he had cleared the ticklers away.

"Now let's eat," he said. "I'm starved."

They tore open the paper sack and spread it for a table cloth and soon were feasting on their fried chicken, bread and butter sandwiches, and juicy tomatoes. Before they were ready for their cake, ants discovered it, and they rescued it just in time.

"I'll never know how ants do it," Freddie said. "Here's a piece of cake, miles from any other cake. It's the first time a piece of cake has ever been here, and probably the last time it ever will be. But in ten minutes' time the ants have discovered it."

"Yes," Chris agreed, munching a drumstick. "They'll do it every time. They must have some sort of built-in radar equipment. One thing sure, let's eat all our food ourselves and not leave any for them!"

After they had eaten, the boys were too contented and too drowsy to talk. One of the nice things about Freddie, Chris thought, was that you didn't have to be always talking with him. You could be quiet and think your own thoughts.

The boys sat that way now, quiet and comfortable, companionable as two cats.

It was very hot. There was not a bit of breeze. The

leaves of the mesquite hung straight down, motionless, and even the weeds seemed to droop. In the south, clouds were piling up for a thunderstorm. Their dazzling brightness made Chris blink.

Freddie stretched himself on the ground full length, though that put his legs in the sunshine. "I'm so sleepy I just have to take a nap," he murmured. "You watch the turkeys while I sleep, and then it will be your turn."

"Okay," Chris said.

Freddie put his hat over his face, and in a few minutes Chris could tell that he was asleep.

Chris leaned against the trunk of the mesquite and watched the turkeys. They fed quietly. Nothing bothered them. Not even a buzzard circled in the sky. The only sounds were the steady drowsy hum of a thousand unseen insects and the gentle gobbling and whistling of the turkeys.

It was all very peaceful and pleasant, but somehow Chris began thinking of his problem again. He didn't want to spoil his afternoon worrying, but Dad would be home tomorrow. Chris felt he had to decide before then.

Dad doesn't even know I'm trying to decide, he thought. He thinks it's all settled that we'll stay here. And really, why shouldn't it be? Somebody's going to be hurt whether we go or stay. Why does it have to be me? Dad's older. I've had to change schools for seven years.

I've never had a chance to have a real true friend before. Why do I have to give him up now? Why can't Dad stay here for just six more years till I finish high school? Then he can go anywhere he wants to.

It would be easier for him to stay here than for me to change schools. This is a good town. Dad can play golf and go swimming. There are plenty of fishing and hunting places. And Margaret will keep a nice house for him. In a little while he'll forget all about the other job. We'll all be happy here. Why don't I just keep still and call it settled?

It all seemed reasonable and true. But Chris knew the real truth was that Dad would feel defeated if he didn't take the promotion.

In spite of knowing this, Chris let his imagination build a dream house in Oakdale. It was a pretty white house, roomy and comfortable, with flowers blooming around it. From this house he and Dad would go to work and school, to hunt and fish and swim and play baseball and golf, and they would return to find Margaret waiting for them.

It was a happy picture, and it almost persuaded Chris, but not entirely. He felt guilty without quite knowing why. There was something that nagged at his mind, something that wouldn't let things stay settled.

Freddie awakened and sat up, stretching. "Did you

see anything?" he asked, between yawns.

"Not a thing. Not a sign of man or beast," Chris answered.

"Well, it's your turn now. You nap while I watch."

Chris didn't feel drowsy any more, but he lay down and covered his face with his hat. It smelled strongly of cheap straw and made him think for a moment of a ship from Havana he had once boarded in Corpus Christi. But in a moment his thoughts were back in Oakdale, worrying again.

He felt uncomfortable, so uncomfortable that he found himself squirming and scratching.

"Fretting about something?" asked Freddie. "Or did the redbugs get you too?"

And then Chris realized that it was not only his problem that was making him uncomfortable. He threw the hat aside and sat up. "I reckon that's what it is," he said and began scratching his ankles.

"We should have put sulphur in our shoes," Freddie said. "Might have known we'd collect thousands of redbugs walking through the pasture. But it's too late now. We'll just have to scratch till we take our baths tonight. Mom has some good lotion we can put on then."

"I wish that time was now," said Chris. "Look, the turkeys are a lot farther away."

"Yes, they've grazed away from us. We'd better

131

move closer to them. You bring the thermos, will you? We'd better sneak over, in case the thief is near."

The boys crept from mesquite to weeds to cactus until they reached another mesquite close to the turkeys. The sun blazed mercilessly, but in the south, thunderheads were boiling up.

"I'm ready for some water," said Freddie. "Sure glad Mom thought of the thermos."

"Me too," said Chris.

Both boys drank till the thermos was empty.

"Let's talk," said Chris. He wanted to quit thinking about Dad.

"Let's," said Freddie. "I've been thinking about what we're going to buy with our PAL money."

"Guns," said Chris. "I thought we were each going to save up for a real gun."

"We are," agreed Freddie, "but what kind of gun? A Remington or a Winchester? A rifle or a shotgun? What gauge? There's a lot to decide."

And the boys were off on a long discussion of guns. But all the time their eyes were alert for any movement in the pasture that might mean the approach of the thief. They saw nothing. The whole countryside was peaceful in the hot sunshine. Even the cattle had grazed out of sight in the other direction. Thunder rumbled faintly in the distance.

132

At last the boys exhausted the subject of guns for the time being and fell quiet.

"This sure is monotonous," said Freddie after a while. "Let's play some kind of game."

"What kind can we play and still keep hidden?"

"How about Tic Tac Toe in the sand?"

"Good idea," Chris agreed.

They cleared a place in the sand and marked off the crisscross spaces and found mesquite twigs to make their O's and X's.

The game proved all too absorbing. They almost forgot to watch the turkeys. "But as soon as anything unusual comes along, my eyes will spot it," Freddie declared. "I've got them trained."

The afternoon breeze sprang up, and it was cooler. The boys, enjoying the relief it brought, hardly noticed that it was stronger than usual and were unaware of the approaching thunderstorm. Suddenly big drops of rain splashed out their Tic Tac Toe.

With the spatter of rain came lightning and thunder. The cloud was almost directly overhead, with blue sky showing all around.

"We'd better get out from under this tree," said Chris. "Looks like we're going to have a real thunderstorm."

"This tree?" Freddie scoffed. "This is more like a

bush than a tree. But we might as well get out from under it. We're getting wet here anyway."

They walked out to a clear place and stood there, backs to the pelting rain, like cattle, drenched and cold. It was raining hard by this time. Sheets of the wind-driven rain blotted even the turkeys from their view. Lightning flashed every few seconds, it seemed, and thunder followed close.

Chris felt silly and unprotected standing there in the pasture, but Freddie thought getting caught in the rain was a huge joke. He began to caper about and chant one of the verses he was always making:

"The rain, the rain, it came down hard,
It caught us two dopes off our guard.
Have we sense enough to stay out of the rain?
No, we haven't got a brain!"

He looked so funny dancing with rain streaming from his face and bouncing from his body that Chris had to laugh.

Then came a more brilliant flash of lightning, with thunder crashing almost immediately. The storm was directly over them. Both boys stood still and waited. The next lightning and thunder were definitely farther away, the next still farther. The storm was rolling rapidly past. In a few minutes the boys stood in sunshine again and

134

watched the rain fall like a receding curtain toward the farm house.

"Well, that sure cooled things off and stopped the redbugs from itching," said Chris, shivering a little in the wind that still blew.

"Sure did. How are our turkeys doing?"

They were feeding as calmly as if it hadn't rained a drop. Now and then one flapped its wings to shake off raindrops and then went back to its busy scratching and pecking.

"A thief could have grabbed a dozen turkeys during the rain and we couldn't have seen him," said Chris.

"Or heard him, either. It would have been a perfect time. I guess our turkey-watching for the day is over. We can't sit down in this mud, and if we stand up, the thief can spot us. We might as well go home."

"It's almost time for the turkeys to go home anyway, isn't it?" Chris asked.

"Yes. Besides, I feel so messy in these wet clothes I want to get into something dry. I'm steaming in this sun."

"Me too," Chris agreed, and the boys picked up their guns and the thermos and started home.

That night when they were bathed and lotioned and in bed with the lights out, Chris closed his eyes and saw again the pasture passing slowly before him, patches of grass and cactus, ant hills and gopher holes. But gradually that picture faded away and in its place was Dad's face again, still with the worried look.

Chris had to talk about it.

"Freddie, are you asleep?" he asked softly.

"No," Freddie answered. " 'Freddie, are you asleep?' " he mimicked playfully. "How could I have answered yes, you dope?"

"No kidding," said Chris. "I've got a secret to tell you."

"What is it?"

"My dad's going to marry Miss Mayes." He lay stiff, waiting to hear what Freddie would say.

Freddie whistled softly. "You mean you're going to have a teacher for a stepmother?"

"Not just any teacher. Margaret Mayes. I bet she'll be a good one."

"It seems a little funny at first, but I bet she will be a good one. You're lucky!"

Chris relaxed. "Thank you, Freddie," he said proudly. "I guess I am."

They lay in silence for a few minutes. Then, "I know something else," said Chris. "We may get to live in Oak-dale."

"Oh, boy, that's swell. Now we can go on with PAL's and play baseball and everything!"

"Yes, but it's just maybe. Maybe Dad will have to

136

leave any day now, and I'll have to go with him."

"Leave any day?" asked Freddie, sounding wide awake for the first time. "Leave? Before Field Day? I never thought of that! Just when we're having so much fun! That would be a howling shame!"

"I know," said Chris slowly. "But I might have to."

"Couldn't you do something about it? Couldn't you beg your dad to stay?"

"I might."

"Well, do that. There's lots of jobs around here he could get. Or I know! If he doesn't want to stay, get him to let you stay! You can live with me!"

"Live with you?" Chris asked doubtfully.

"Sure. No kidding. I mean it."

"I don't know whether your folks would want me to."

"Sure they would. They like you. And Mom's all the time saying that with five kids one more makes no difference."

"It would sure be fun, but I don't know if I'd want to live away from Dad. Especially with Miss Mayes coming to live with us. That would be fun too."

"Not as much fun as baseball and hunting and fishing with me. I don't want you to leave. Come live with me, Oily. No fooling, I think you'd make a swell brother!"

Freddie meant it! He really meant that he wanted Chris for a brother! The knowledge filled Chris with pride and wonder. He lay in the dark, smiling with happiness. Suddenly he felt strong and confident. He felt the way he'd felt the first time he walked without crutches after he broke his leg.

And Chris knew his problem was solved. He was a little dizzy from the swiftness of it. He felt like a swing that has been twisted around and around till the ropes were tight as a spring, then turned loose to whirl and spin back to its natural position. All his worry was gone, and he felt free and glad.

It all happened so quickly that Freddie didn't even notice Chris's silence. He had no idea that a momentous change had taken place in Chris's heart. "And Mom's cooking," he was going on persuasively. "How would you like to eat Mom's cooking every day? Don't forget Mom's cooking!"

Chris laughed a little. "I can't forget it," he said. "I wish I had some right now!"

"Let's," said Freddie, hopping out of bed. "We're guerrillas making a raid on enemy supplies," he whispered, leading the way down the dark hall. "Watch out for the third step. It creaks."

Chris laughed and joked as he ate his midnight snack. He was no longer worried about his problem. All he needed now was a chance to tell Dad of his decision.

12

Unexpected Holiday

Monday morning on the way to the school bus Chris suggested a detour. "Let's run the traps before we go to school. It's my last chance for a week," he said.

"We won't have time for all of them," Freddie decided. "But we can go to the closest one if we run part of the way."

Freddie got his gun, and they set out for the trap at a dogtrot, the dew-wet grass slapping at their ankles and drenching the bottoms of their blue jeans. When they came near the trap, they could see something in it, something struggling.

"We'll have to kill it," Freddie said, loading his gun.

Then, as Chris followed him closely, he cried, "Hold everything! It's a skunk!"

But the skunk did not hold everything. It let its weapon fly before the boys were quite out of reach.

"Phew!" exclaimed Chris, continuing to run. "It's lucky we weren't any closer!"

"We were too close as it was," Freddie said. "Fresh air, do your work!"

He shot the skunk, and the boys ran to the bus stop. Freddie stopped just long enough to cache his gun under the chaparral bush where he usually hid it when he wanted to hunt on his way home from school.

The boys climbed aboard the bus breathlessly. Before they had gone a mile, some of the girls began clamoring for the rest of the windows to be opened. "It's terribly stuffy in here," they insisted.

Even with all the windows open, it was not pleasant. "Smells like something dead in here," the boy behind Chris and Freddie complained.

The high-school boy across the aisle said, "Smells like a polecat to me. Did you two kids have a run-in with one of our little white-striped friends?"

"Yes," they admitted sheepishly.

"You're sure going to be popular in school today!" he promised them, with gleeful malice.

Outside on the school grounds, it was not so bad.

But after fifteen minutes in the classroom, the odor was disagreeably noticeable, even though all the windows were open. At first everyone politely ignored it, but soon the less elegant boys began holding their noses and pantomiming nausea. Nell, petticoat showing, slipped up to Miss Mayes's desk. "May I move?" she asked. "Chris smells bad."

Just then Cotton blared out, "Miss Mayes, something near me stinks!"

"Cotton!" Miss Mayes reproved him. But something had to be done. "Class, we may as well face the fact that there is a very disagreeable smell in the room," she said. "If anyone has brought anything bad-smelling into the room, he must take it out at once. It isn't funny."

There was a moment of silence. Chris sat embarrassed, wondering what to do. Just as he raised his hand, Jack blurted out, "It's Chris."

"It's me too," said Freddie. "We got too close to a skunk."

"Oh," said Miss Mayes. "Well, there's only one thing I know to do. If you stay here, we'll all feel sick the rest of the day. The best thing you can do is to go home until the odor wears off."

Chris looked at his shoes. He wanted to sink through the floor. To be sent home from school! The disgrace of it! Just when he thought things were going so well, too!

He glanced at Freddie. Freddie was strapping his books together, smiling.

"He's putting on a brave front," Chris thought. "If he can, I can too." He began selecting the books to take home.

"Freddie," Miss Mayes remembered, "you live in the country. Can your folks come for you?"

"I'll go home with Chris," Freddie said.

"But phone them when you get there," Miss Mayes insisted. "And both of you take a good soapy bath and put on clean clothes, and wash the clothes you have on. Use plenty of soap."

"Yes, ma'am," both boys promised.

"Here's a note explaining to Mr. Elson. Leave it in the office on your way out."

Chris held his head high, and he felt a stiff grin on his face. But he was miserably embarrassed as they walked out.

"What's your dad going to say about this?" he asked Freddie when they had left school. "Mine isn't going to like it."

"Oh, he won't say anything. I've been too close to skunks before. It's my mom who isn't going to like it. It's a nuisance to get the clothes smelling clean again."

"I've never been sent home from school before," said Chris. "My dad isn't going to like it."

"Don't feel so bad about it, Chris," Freddie advised. "We didn't do anything bad. We didn't break any rules or anything. It wasn't our fault we got sprayed."

"Dad'll say we should have had better judgment than to get so close to a skunk. He'll say we should have gone straight to the school bus."

"Well," said Freddie cheerfully, "crying won't help spilled milk. We're out of school for the day, so we might as well make the most of it and have fun."

"Well, yes," said Chris. "I hadn't thought of that. We do have a free day. What shall we do?"

"I'll phone Mom to come and get us. Then we can go on watching the turkeys."

"Oh, sure," Chris agreed. "It's a perfect opportunity. Why didn't I think of it?"

When they reached his house, Chris began stripping for his bath while Freddie telephoned.

"Freddie Felsing," his mother exclaimed when she had heard his story, "if you're not a bother! And me in the middle of hanging out my washing! You'll just have to wait until I get through."

"Okay, Mom," Freddie agreed. "We'll start walking and meet you."

While Freddie took his turn in the tub, Chris, comfortable in clean clothes, sat and thought about their predicament. "A friend sure makes a difference," he con-

143

cluded. "Trouble isn't half as bad when you have a friend to share it."

By the time they had squeezed Freddie into some of Chris's clothes and laughed at the way he bulged out of them, Chris was almost as light-hearted as Freddie.

They stuffed their smelly clothes into two pillow cases. "No use to wash them here in the bathtub," Freddie decided. "Mom can throw them in the washing machine. Besides they'd be heavy to carry wet."

Chris wrote a note for Dad. Then each boy made himself a ham and cheese sandwich to eat on the way and set out for Freddie's, their pillow sacks of clothes slung across their shoulders but their school books forgotten.

It seemed strange to walk along streets where only babies played, strange and somehow exciting. It was strange and exciting to walk on the highway when they got out of town. Not many cars passed them. One man stopped and asked suspiciously what two boys were doing walking the highway instead of being in school. Another stopped and, recognizing Freddie, offered a lift, but Freddie explained and declined.

They had not walked much more than a mile when Mrs. Felsing picked them up. "Phooie!" she said as they climbed into the car.

"It's not so much us any more," Freddie assured her.

"Now since we've had a bath, it's mostly our clothes. We have them in these sacks."

"Oh, you're just used to each other," she replied. "You needn't think you're going to perfume up my clean house!"

Chris knew she was only teasing, and of course Freddie did too. "Don't worry," Freddie said. "We don't want to stay in your old house. We're going out turkey-watching again."

"Oh?"

"Yes. So if you'll just fix us a good lunch, we'll be out of your way just as much as if we were in school."

"And for that I'll be grateful!"

13

Rewards

They stayed in the house only long enough for Freddie to change into his own more comfortable clothes and for Mrs. Felsing to pack their lunch. Then they sprinkled sulphur around their ankles and set out to look for the turkeys. Chris carried Freddie's BB gun and Freddie his father's .22.

"Have you shot that .22 much?" Chris asked.

"Sure, Daddy's let me shoot it many a time."

"Does he let you take it by yourself like this?"

"Well, no, he never has. But I've never asked him, so he hasn't said no, either. And I got to thinking that if our thief is a wolf or a bobcat or even a big old coon, we'll need something stronger than a BB gun to kill him."

They walked through the flowery pasture and the next one without a sign of the turkeys. "We'll cut across to the creek pasture," Freddie decided. "Maybe we'll find them there."

The turkeys were in the creek pasture, feeding in an open space just this side of an oak motte. "Thank goodness they're near shade today," said Freddie. "This is going to be another scorcher. We'll cross over and watch from the shade of the trees."

"We'll be closer to the turkeys when we're in the motte, and better hidden, too," Chris said. "We can climb up in one of the trees, and the thief won't know there's anyone within miles."

"Good idea," Freddie agreed. "We'll do that."

They crossed over to the motte and found a tree with two broad branches facing in the right direction for watching the turkeys. They laid their guns near the foot of the tree and climbed up with their sacks of food. They judged by the shadows that it was time for lunch.

It was fun eating in the tree, leaning far out to pass sandwiches and deviled eggs and potato chips back and forth and balancing their bottled drinks in the forks of the branches.

It was much cooler up in the tree than it had been yesterday under the mesquite. There was no chance for napping today, but plenty of time for talking. "Perching up here in the tree makes me feel romantic," Freddie said, striking a lovesick pose. "Let's talk about girls."

Freddie had a girl, pretty black-eyed Mary Belle Anson, who thought he was wonderful. Chris didn't have a girl — didn't want one — but Freddie thought he should have one. They talked for a long time about girls that Freddie said sort of liked Chris, trying to find one that was as sweet as Mary Belle.

They discussed this fascinating subject so eagerly that they almost forgot to watch the turkeys. But at last they tired of it and turned to baseball. They analyzed the strength and weakness of each member of their team and Jack's and tried to work out the strategy for meeting Jack's team on Field Day. They felt sure their team would win.

Somehow both boys avoided the subject of Chris's leaving Oakdale or staying with Freddie.

By midafternoon they were cramped from sitting in the tree and climbed down to stretch.

"We're sure earning our reward," said Chris. "This watching and waiting is harder than marking the turkeys was." He turned a somersault to flex his muscles.

"Well, I don't know," Freddie disagreed. "This is boring, but not hard."

"I'd rather be doing something. Think of all the good

time we're wasting just sitting here. We could be fishing or hunting or playing catch."

"You won't mind when we collect the reward."

They started playing Tic-Tac-Toe again. Soon they were so interested in their match that they forgot all about the turkeys.

Suddenly they heard a great gobbling. They whirled to look.

"There!" cried Chris, pointing. "See?"

"Where?" asked Freddie, grabbing the .22 and loading it.

"There, heading toward the creek! See, it's a big wolf with a turkey in its mouth!"

Freddie wasted no breath in answering. He sighted the wolf, which by this time was some distance away, and fired. Once, twice, three times. The third time he hit the wolf. It fell to the ground.

The boys raced past the disturbed flock to the wolf and then approached it cautiously for fear it might be only injured with enough strength left to attack them. But it was dead, still clutching a half-grown turkey in its jaws.

"Hurray!" shouted Freddie. "Fifty dollars, come to Freddie!"

"Golly, it's a big one!" Chris said.

"You've got your gun. We're ready to start for home.

Let's take the wolf to show Daddy."

"Won't that run into a lot of trouble?"

"Not too much. Anyway, trouble or not, it's what I want to do."

So they took the wolf home all the way across the pastures, sometimes dragging it, sometimes carrying it between them, Freddie holding the front feet, Chris the back. It was a hot, disagreeable job, and several times Chris was ready to quit. "This wolf smells worse than the turkeys," he said. "I didn't know earning the reward would be such a smelly business. The combination of wolf and skunk isn't doing us any good, either."

But Freddie could not be persuaded to leave the wolf. "I want to prove it to Daddy," he insisted. "Besides, I want to take some pictures."

At last they reached the cow lot. "Daddy," Freddie shouted, "where are you?"

"Here in the tool shed," Mr. Felsing shouted back.

The boys heaved the wolf into carrying position again with a final burst of energy. They took it over to where Mr. Felsing was working and with a heave and a ho threw the animal down before the door of the tool shed.

Mr. Felsing whistled. "So the thief was a wolf, after all," he said, "and in broad daylight. I wouldn't have believed it."

"It was carrying a turkey away when I shot it, going towards the creek."

"It must have a den of young ones it was feeding, probably somewhere along the creek bank. We'll have to find that den and clean it out."

"Oh, Daddy, let's go wolf hunting tonight!"

"Can't tonight. I have a meeting in town. Besides, we want to wait until Clem Dickerson and his wolf-hounds can go with us. It'll take dogs to do the job right."

"But can we go with you when you do go?"

"Sure. I guess you've earned that."

Mrs. Felsing and the girls came out and looked at the wolf, shuddering but admiring.

"Speaking of earning," Freddie said, not to be side-tracked, "we've sure earned our reward."

"What reward?" asked Mr. Felsing.

"The fifty dollars you promised us for finding the thief."

"Fifty dollars? What fifty dollars?"

Chris held his breath.

"Now, Daddy," Freddie began.

Mr. Felsing laughed. "I'll write you a check as soon as we go in the house."

"Two checks, one for Chris and one for me."

"Mine for twenty dollars and Freddie's for thirty." Chris said.

"Make it twenty-seven fifty and twenty-two fifty," Freddie said generously. "Only half the licking was for going to the Frends'. The other half was for not being dependable."

"I don't know what you're talking about," said Mr. Felsing, "but anything you say is all right with me, just so long as it adds up to fifty."

Chris's father drove up and called to him just as they were going in the house. He got out of the car and walked over to them. "Hi, everybody," he said. "Well, Chris, I must say you have a mighty happy face for a boy who's been sent home from school."

The smile faded from Chris's face.

"Now, Mr. Gregory," Mrs. Felsing said quickly, "you mustn't blame Chris for that!"

"Getting sent home from school is pretty serious," Dad said.

"If I'd known about the skunk this morning, I never would have let them go to school in the first place. Getting caught by a skunk isn't bad; happens to Freddie regular at least once a year. It's just part of a boy's growing up in the country. So you mustn't blame Chris."

"Well," said Dad, "if you're sure that's all it was — no sassy wisecracks or anything."

"Oh, no, sir," both boys assured him earnestly.

"Then okay, Chris," Dad said, with a pat on his

shoulder. "How did this wolf get here?"

"That's what the boys are looking so happy about," Mr. Felsing said, "and they've got a right to be happy about it."

They told Dad the whole story then, and he was duly impressed. He congratulated the boys and praised their perseverance. Then he said it was time to go home.

Alone in the car with Dad, Chris was eager to tell of his new decision about leaving Oakdale. But it wasn't as easy as he had thought it would be. Somehow he felt timid about bringing up the subject.

Dad was chatting idly, asking questions about the turkey adventure. Chris answered with only half a mind, trying to think of some way to bring up the subject of leaving. Finally Dad stopped talking, and they rode in silence for a few minutes. Still Chris could not think of a way to open the conversation. He decided to plunge right into the middle of it.

"Dad," he announced, "I think you ought to take that promotion."

Dad looked at him quickly. "You do?" he asked. "Why, Son?"

"I just do," said Chris, "that's all."

"Why?" Dad asked again.

"Well, I don't think you'd like selling leases very much."

They were both speaking slowly, pausing to find the right words. Chris had the queer feeling that it was a conversation in slow motion.

"I thought it was settled that we would stay," said Dad.

"I thought so, too, at first. But I've changed my mind."

"Why, Chris?"

"Dad," Chris asked in sudden panic, "you can still take the promotion, can't you? It isn't too late for that, is it?"

"No, it's not too late. I can still take the promotion."

"Whee!" said Chris. "I was scared for a minute."

Dad turned off the highway and parked the car at the crest of a little hill. The sunset glow was still in the sky, but dusk was creeping over the town and here and there lights were beginning to twinkle.

Dad turned sideways to face Chris, leaning against the door. Chris sat looking straight ahead.

"Tell me about it, Son," Dad said quietly.

"I don't know if I can. It's sort of hard to put into words. I just don't think you'd be very happy here."

"Chris, you know I can't be happy anywhere unless you're happy, don't you?"

"That's just it, Dad. I don't have to stay here to be happy."

154

"You don't? But you've been telling me that you want to stay here, that you've even been praying we wouldn't have to leave."

"I know. But that was before I found out something. I'm not afraid to leave Oakdale any more. I found it out all of a sudden, when Freddie invited me to live with him."

"But I thought you wanted to stay here to be with Freddie."

"I do. But Freddie's sort of the cause why I found out I can go."

"Do you mean you've had a quarrel? Do you mean your friendship is ended?"

"Oh, no! We're better friends than ever. I'm not saying it right. I guess I mean that Freddie's the reason I'm not afraid to leave."

"What do you mean?"

"Well, Freddie chose me to be his friend. And Freddie's tops! He could have anybody in school for his best friend, and they'd be proud. But he chose me, and we get along swell. He even wants me to live with him. So — don't you see — that sort of gives me faith in myself. If he likes me, I can't be so bad. I'm not afraid to face a new bunch of kids again. Maybe there'll be another boy there that will be a good friend. If not, I'll still have Freddie."

"But Freddie won't be with you. He'll be in another town."

"I know, but that won't make too much difference. That's the thing I found out. You don't have to see your friend every day to keep on being friends. I bet if we didn't see each other for five years, we'd still be friends."

"You've got something there, Son."

"Do you understand what I mean, Dad? Of course I'd like to stay here and pal around with Freddie. But it isn't *necessary*. Besides, I can visit him, and he can visit me, and we can write to each other. We'll still have good times together. But all that's why I think you ought to take the promotion, Dad. I think that would be best for us. Do you see?"

Dad put an arm around Chris and hugged him close. "Yes, Chris," he said, "I do see. And I'm proud of you. You thought our problem through, and you've made the right decision. You're brave and wise and unselfish. Chris, I can't tell you how proud and happy I am to have you for my son."

Dad's voice was husky, and Chris felt his own throat tighten with tears. "Aw, Dad," was all he could say.

"There's one thing I can do to make it easier for you," Dad said. "You won't have to miss Field Day. I'll have to leave by the end of this week, but I'll arrange for you to stay here the three weeks until school is out."

"Good," said Chris. "I can stay with Freddie."

"Maybe," said Dad. "And Margaret will look out for you, I know. We'll work out something."

They sat in silence for a minute, watching the lights of the town twinkle like fireflies. Then Dad switched on the ignition. "Let's go," he said. "Let's go tell Margaret."

Chris realized suddenly that this was the first time Dad had asked him to go with him to see Margaret.

"Yes," he agreed, smiling with happiness, "let's go tell Margaret."